KINDU

*A Kindu warrior ran out of one of the houses, clutch-
ing a pile of clothing to his bare chest . . . Two
screaming white women: one of them already naked,
the other having her clothes ripped off her by two
grinning Kindu warriors . . . Ten dead men lying
face up in a row in the front yard, each shot through
the head . . . Two small children running, pointing and
opening their mouths wide in silent screaming . . .*

Sheriff had seen rapes before, and he had killed rapists. He had watched young children weeping over the
corpses of their slaughtered parents. Cruelty wasn't
confined to the Kindu. But what came next Michael
Sheriff had not seen ever before . . .

Coming Soon in the
MICHAEL SHERIFF: THE SHIELD series

ARABIAN ASSAULT
ISLAND INTRIGUE

MICHAEL SHERIFF: THE SHIELD

AFRICAN ASSIGNMENT

PRESTON MacADAM

AVON
PUBLISHERS OF BARD, CAMELOT, DISCUS AND FLARE BOOKS

MICHAEL SHERIFF: THE SHIELD—AFRICAN ASSIGN-
MENT is an original publication of Avon Books. This work has
never before appeared in book form. This work is a novel. Any similarity to actual persons or events is purely coincidental.

AVON BOOKS
A division of
The Hearst Corporation
1790 Broadway
New York, New York 10019

Copyright © 1985 by Preston MacAdam
Published by arrangement with the author
Library of Congress Catalog Card Number: 84-091655
ISBN: 0-380-89687-7

First Avon Printing, June 1985

AVON TRADEMARK REG. U. S. PAT. OFF. AND IN OTHER
COUNTRIES, MARCA REGISTRADA, HECHO EN U. S. A.

Printed in the U. S. A.

WFH 10 9 8 7 6 5 4 3 2 1

For Daddy's Little Boy

1

THE LAND ROVER bumped and swayed its halting way over the jungle road. It was really little more than a path—and sometimes not even as much as that—barely wide enough to accommodate the four-wheel-drive vehicle. The three Caucasian passengers stared alertly into the dense foliage on either side of them. Almost anyone else would have taken note of the deep verdancy of the foliage and the occasional flashes of color that were birds or spots of brilliant flowers, but these men saw only that there were thousands of places for enemies to secrete themselves. In the loud chattering and screeching of disturbed animals, the men only listened for the stealthiness of those who might try to kill them. The Kindu lands, to all the rest of the world, seemed remote and protected behind these walls of tropical forest, but the three Caucasians knew that danger and death lurked everywhere.

They conversed with one another occasionally, in a strange Slavic tongue that their black driver had never heard before. It was certainly not the language of the old colonial masters, nor of the American hunters who sometimes came to Leikawa to hunt game. It was guttural and the sounds alien and unpleasant.

It was Czech.

The faces of the three men were brightly sunburned. The redness of their skin betrayed their recent arrival to this part of the country. In Europe it was the dead of winter. They swatted at insects, grunted at each heavy jolt of the Land Rover. They had not once made a friendly gesture to the driver. They had scarcely taken any notice of him at all, except once, to check him for weapons, taking away his single holstered pistol.

The trio wore khaki clothing of American manufacture. But even though the clothes were obviously of recent purchase, still showing the factory's sharp creases, they were already filthy with perspiration and the excretions of the jungle.

Lukas Paloucky, the leader of the Czechs, was a big man over six feet tall and weighing well over two hundred pounds. He took a metal flask from his hip pocket and drank deeply from the liquor inside. Paloucky didn't offer the alcohol to his mates, but before he could return it to his pocket, the second Czech reached over and slipped it out of his grasp, and drank greedily from it.

This second man was just as tall, but slender. Like a seasoned warrior, Otokar Hron showed the scars of many battles. Two fingers of his left hand were missing. The deep scarlet lines on his face stood in marked contrast to the rest of his exposed flesh. Even though he was red from the sun, the fairness of Hron's complexion was obvious against the old, but still angry, wounds.

The third Czech—Jurek Theer—took the flask and raised it to his lips. It was empty. He flung it away in disgust. It would have been lost in the jungle had not Paloucky reached up and grasped it out of the air with a sure, mechanical motion.

The third man was, so far as the driver was concerned, the most frightening of the Europeans. There was a . . . menace about him. *Menace*, in the Kindu tongue, referred to animals that killed mercilessly, in the night.

Jurek Theer's hair was somewhat darker than his companions'. While they were a sort of dirty blond, the thin hair on his head was closer to a genuine brown. A thick moustache covering his mouth was shot through with discoloring gray. His eyes seemed to regard the whole world with loathing. The driver had not once seen Theer smile, nor relax the set, disgruntled expression that occupied all the muscles of his face.

The Czechs began to argue. Probably about the flask, the driver assumed. They might have been comrades, but they apparently had no great liking for one another. Though he didn't understand a word they spoke, from the tone of their voices the driver learned much.

They carried big guns, and there were more weapons in the wooden boxes that lay on the floor of the Land Rover. The three men made much of themselves, of their size, and of their experience. But the driver knew them for cowards. It was fear that made them so dangerous. The driver spat out the window. He hoped the chief had good reason to bring such men into the realm of the Kindu.

The road suddenly widened, and leveled out in a large clearing that still showed the stubble of the jungle in the fields on either side. Wretchedly clothed natives listlessly tilled the earth with ancient wood-and-stone tools long given up in almost every other part of the world. Women bent with their bare breasts dangling over the shallow dusty furrows. Men clad in ragged loincloths dug the ground with crude hoes. Groups of young children, completely naked, crawled through the dust in groups, weeding.

Every one of the field workers looked malnourished.

It was apparent why. None of the United Nations resolutions on slavery had reached this forgotten pocket of African cruelty. The field workers were slaves, pure and simple.

Black men in light brown military uniforms swaggered along the perimeter of the field, guns slung over their shoulders, the long black thongs of their whips trailing in the dust.

The smug guards saluted the Land Rover as it roared past; the slaves in the field scarcely glanced up.

The Land Rover passed by a clump of mud hovels beyond the fields. These were obviously the abodes of the workers. The road became smoother. Now and then there were low concrete buildings, whitewashed to a startling brilliancy, some of them with doors painted bright red or blue. These were the homes of the powerful of the Kindu, who had become rich on the profits of slavery, extortion, murder, and bribery.

The Land Rover stopped in a large earthen square, fronted on all four sides by substantial concrete buildings. There was no fountain, no statue, no marker, no indication of art or civilization at all—yet this was the center of the Kindu culture. Beneath outjutting grass roofs, a dusty bazaar stretched along two sides of the square. Sullen women and old men sold liquor, tattered clothing, battered domestic utensils, and rotting food.

On the shady side of the square, on a slightly elevated concrete platform painted purple and edged with long strips of soiled red carpeting, a black man sat squarely in the middle of a low American upholstered couch. Huge epaulets stood on his shoulders. A mass of glittering medals crowned either side of his chest. Dark glasses hid his eyes. A bright red beret was perched atop the mass of his thick black hair.

The three Europeans climbed out of the Land Rover and approached this rural potentate, whose sophistication lay only in his ruthlessness and cultivated cruelty. They stepped forward without either insolence or trepidation.

Lukas Paloucky nodded to the African on his low throne.

"Do you have them?" the black man asked in French, the only language they had in common.

"Yes."

"Show me."

The leader of the Caucasians glanced over his shoulder at his two followers, and muttered something in Czech.

Hron and Theer protested, and waved toward the black men who had begun to gather along the edges of the hot, dusty town square. They saw no reason the Kindu shouldn't do the heavy work.

Paloucky yelled once, and only a few words.

With no more complaints, Hron and Theer returned to the Land Rover, lugged out one of the heavy crates from the vehicle, and dropped it on the ground between Paloucky and the African chief.

Hron, his sweat gathering in the deep scars of his face, returned to the Land Rover, and brought back a hammer and a crowbar.

For several moments the only sound to be heard in that vast square, with by now several hundred persons present, was the hammering of the crowbar, and then the harsh metallic screaking of the nails as the top of the box was pried open.

The lid of the box fell to the side, sending up a cloud of acrid yellow dust.

When the dust cleared, the sun glinted on two dozen new rifles.

The Kindu leader stood from his couch and stepped with purpose to the very edge of the dais. He peered over into the box.

"Show me," he said again.

Paloucky leaned over and picked up one of the rifles. He took a metal clip from his belt and forced it in the underbelly of the wood and metal weapon. "It's an AK-47," he said. "They all are." He moved a couple of levers. The gun was entirely at home in his hands; he held it the way a truck driver holds a steering wheel, with perfect ease and knowledge.

"Show me," the black leader repeated.

The Czech turned and glanced around the square. Most of the gathered crowd was Kindu, the men in the same khaki uniform as their leader, and the women in a characteristic sacklike robe of coarse purple cloth. Among them, however, were other blacks, distinguished by their ragged colorless clothes and their general air of downtroddenness. They were the servants and the slaves of the Kindu.

On the outskirts of the square, three small boys stood together. None of them was more than ten years old. Their bellies were distended with hunger and their skin showed the whitish welts of many beatings. One listed heavily to the left on a shriveled leg.

The boys, mystified by the arrival of the white men,

stared with unabashed curiosity at the Czechs and the box of gleaming rifles.

Paloucky barely took time to aim. Even if he had, the knot of servant boys wouldn't have understood what he was doing. Then, with a single pop, the rifle bucked sharply against his shoulder and sent invisible death flying through the air. The crippled boy was lifted up off the ground and sent sprawling a dozen yards into a shady alley between concrete buildings. He fell dead without even a twitch, his shriveled leg bent at an acute angle away from his inert body.

The remaining two boys stood in shocked and unbelieving silence. They stared down at the empty space where a second before their friend had stood and laughed between them. His final footprints were still marked in the sand. While every instinct told them to run, they remained utterly paralyzed. They wanted to cry, but their faces were frozen in horror. The necessity to survive made them want to fall to their knees and plead for life, but they were hypnotized by the rifle that had so expeditiously dispatched their playmate.

Only when Paloucky casually lowered the rifle did their animal senses take control again and they ran, squalling and hysterical, from the plaza.

The chief seemed unimpressed. He stepped down from the dais and slowly made his way toward the body of the dead boy. He stopped at the mouth of the alley.

The dead boy lay staring up into the sun. Flies were already clustered thick and black around his open mouth, so many of them it looked as if his lips were moving and he were trying to speak.

"So," said the chief, "it will kill a child."

Paloucky and his two soldiers stood behind the chief. They said nothing.

"Will it kill a man?" the chief asked sarcastically.

The Czech nodded.

The chief stepped nearer the boy's corpse, and pointed at the tiny black wound in the crippled child's forehead.

"Such a little hole," said the chief, still trying to downplay the rifle's power.

The Czech walked around the chief, reached down and took the dead boy's arm. In one swift motion, he flipped the corpse over on its face.

There was no back to the boy's head.

His brain lay in a welter of blood and shattered bone in the yellow dust.

The bullet, once it had entered through its minute point of contact, had exploded in the child's head.

"You killed a servant," said the chief, in a weak attempt to gain back some ground.

"He was a cripple," Paloucky answered impassively. "You would have starved him anyway."

For the first time the black man smiled. He shrugged his shoulders and then walked away.

2

AFTER THE British Airways jumbo jet had landed at Boston's Logan Airport, Michael Sheriff endured customs. He was no longer connected with the CIA and received no special treatment here. Of course, when the occasion demanded, there were a hundred ways to ignore borders, guards, searches, and delays. But the Indian mission, for all its complexity and importance, had been merely routine. Sheriff was returning as a casual United States citizen.

"Three months?" the customs officer said curiously. "What the hell did you do in that part of India for three months? Big game?"

"The biggest," said Sheriff, and unlatched one of the steel gun cases.

The officer took one look at the weapons inside, glanced into Sheriff's steely eyes, and nervously waved him through.

He walked with his few bags to the parking garage where he had left his car. He took nothing for granted. Just as he always watched for an attack, even in the most crowded street of a city he had never visited before, in the changing room in an exclusive men's shop, in the shower at a health club he attended under one of his assumed names, so did he always examine his car before he got into it.

The vehicle had been sitting at Logan for weeks. It was an apparently modest Volvo sedan, the same kind of automobile that countless other Boston suburbanites drove. Sheriff had no need to drive anything overtly luxurious or fashionable. A loner, he had no interest in impressing strangers and parking-lot attendants. He only required that a vehicle be absolutely dependable in its performance.

The Volvo's Turbo engine guaranteed greater power and speed than anyone would expect from a sedan. The frame was stronger than usual, thanks to a special order filled at Volvo's home plant in Sweden.

It was not a perfect car. It would never be an armored vehicle to astound his enemies, but it suited Sheriff's purpose. It was actually very much like him—sturdy, faster than necessary, stronger than the competition, not flashy or drawing unnecessary attention to itself, totally trustworthy.

It also had a small bomb under the hood.

Sheriff squatted down in front of the car, reached up under the bumper, and flicked the switch that deactivated the device.

Anyone who attempted to raise the hood in his absence would lose at least an arm; and his entire head might be sheared off. That had happened once, at high noon, under the elevated lanes of Manhattan's West Side Highway. Sheriff very much regretted the loss of that Volvo.

After disconnecting the bomb, Sheriff went through his usual procedure—checking the underside of the car, the trunk, the brakes, and the steering mechanism.

He had no doubt that some very clever operative could have got round all that, but he couldn't spend his entire life worrying. Sheriff didn't expect to die in bed. Someday, sooner or later, someone would get to him. He could take sane steps to make certain that his death wasn't foolish, but he could never guard against all possibilities. There were ten thousand ways that he might die—but there was only one way that he intended to live. When he had checked what he could in five minutes, he drove west on the Massachusetts Turnpike, then headed north onto Route 128.

This expressway swoops around Boston in a wide arc that begins and ends at the Atlantic Ocean. Always at a distance of about ten miles from the core of the city, it was one of the first expressways ever built in America. It was certainly the first to be constructed which did not connect two points with one another. "The Highway to Nowhere," as the critics called it, rose from the sea and swept around through the suburbs of Boston only to disappear back into the water at the end of its long journey.

Rather than a boondoggle that would never be used by the public, Route 128 astounded even its most valiant proponents. It became a magnet for industry and commerce. Now it was called the "Main Street of American Technology." On either side of its ten asphalt lanes grew the headquarters for the new corporations and research firms that would propel this country into the battle for world dominance in the new technological age.

The corporations that were born along Route 128 grew in size and influence. They constructed appropriately large headquarters for themselves as they prospered. Their names and their acronyms have grown out of obscurity to become part of everyday American language. Their concrete and steel and tinted-glass office buildings rival those of any major city in size, architecture, and fame. Route 128 now has traffic jams to rival those of Paris and Rome and New York.

But due west of Boston, not far from where Sheriff turned onto Route 128, stands one large building, constructed of white concrete, which carries no corporate logo, nor has any sign to announce its owner or its tenants. Its stern walls can barely be glimpsed through the denuded trees in winter; in summer it is not visible at all. The structure bears a likeness to the frontier forts of the American West. Its solid facade is sliced only occasionally by long vertical windows that resemble the apertures in the primitive stockades through which the settlers defended themselves. And like those hearty settlers, those inside this building—known familiarly as "The Fort"—are dedicated to the defense of our own civilization from the barbaric hordes that would reduce it to a shattered sphere of chaos and decay.

Even if the hundreds of thousands of casual travelers who passed the building daily knew the name of the company that owned and occupied it, they would only shrug. *Management Information Services* might as well be the name of the building next to it, or across the expressway from it. All such names sound alike, and suggest a company which feeds off government contracts and cash-heavy corporations.

Management Information Services—MIS—is hardly the handle to excite the casual consumer. But in the higher echelons of Wall Street and Zurich and the City of London, in all the capitals of world finance and power-brokering, MIS brings immediate though sometimes grudging respect.

MIS is the court of last resort, an ally of the last hope.

The architecture of its headquarters is no mistake. That fortresslike facade was carefully worked out beforehand, and is always bitterly perceived by those who stagger to its gate in supplication.

MIS is known only to those who need to know of it. To everyone else, it's just another of those damned companies on Route 128 whose employees block up the traffic at rush hour.

It has resources and ability that cannot be obtained anywhere else in the Free World. Inside its thick concrete walls, buried deep in the rocky earth of Massachusetts, is the largest computer system to be found in the world outside the Pentagon. And the system at MIS—it was known—is more up-to-date than the one in Washington.

The mission of MIS isn't to bring civilization and order to a chaotic world. It exists in order to protect the Free World and its supporting institutions from the forces aligned against it—whatever form those forces may take.

By every means at its disposal—and those means are varied and often mysterious—MIS seeks to preserve and perpetuate, both here and abroad, the way of life propounded by the Constitution of the United States.

MIS had sent Michael Sheriff into the wastes of northern India, and MIS would designate his next battlefield.

Yet, when it came down to it, Michael Sheriff had no real fidelity to the company, those three common initials.

Michael Sheriff placed all his trust in one man, the Chairman, the man to whom Sheriff had silently vowed his allegiance.

As head of MIS, the Chairman was more than Sheriff's boss, more than his friend, he was Michael's liege lord. The only man to whom Michael Sheriff afforded total respect, and in whom he reposed perfect trust.

From his office, a corner suite with two narrow windows facing into the deciduous forest surrounding The Fort, the Chairman controlled an empire of information. The office was filled with American art and American antiques—superb and, in some cases, unique examples of colonial craftsmanship. It was chaste and spare, like the Chairman himself, but full of integrity.

Into this office came all the digested knowledge of two hundred experts, covering all fields of human activity. Together they monitored all developments in the world—daily. Three thousand newspapers and periodicals from all over the globe were mercilessly clipped to shreds. Their seemingly random bits of information were entered into a monstrous and elaborate computerized code, and subsequently analyzed, catalogued, and correlated in a hundred thousand different permutations. The Chairman recruited graduates of the best computer-engineering schools in the country, and into their capable, imaginative hands he entrusted the designs of The Fort's massive computer system. They built a network that was almost a full generation ahead of any comparable system in the world, capable of social and economic predictions that would have astounded anyone in the field. Even the computer engineers were sometimes astonished at their successes. MIS amply rewarded them for their work and as yet every one of these men and women had remained unswervingly loyal to the company, or rather to the Chairman. The amazing efficacy of The Fort's computer system had never become known outside MIS. The Chairman's ability to predict world crises and to pinpoint trouble spots seemed almost mystic to the heads of governments. They suspected MIS of all manner of subterfuges. But MIS had no need of paid spies. Information was there for the taking. It was in analysis and prediction that MIS overwhelmed all its competition.

The intelligence-gathering resources of the CIA, the Pentagon, the NSC were all, to a greater or lesser extent, affected by politics—the politics of the man in the Oval Office, the politics of the chiefs of staff, of the cabinet and other high-level government appointees. MIS was affected only by the will of the Chairman, and the Chairman was interested only in clear-sightedness. He had no motive for slanting the truth of the conclusions drawn by his army of researchers and analysts. And for this reason the Chairman and MIS were often right when everyone was proved wrong.

During the last world war, the Chairman had watched with anger and frustration as the multinational corporations had paid one another for the right to kill off Allied and Fascist armies. He had seen German and Japanese corporations become as large, as dangerous, and as evil as the governments that protected them. And later, while the world watched with horror and fascination as the United States, Russia, and China played games of nuclear brinksmanship, the Chairman had leveled his unflinching gaze upon the next arena in the game of global warfare. Very early on he understood the explosion of technology that would be triggered by the rapid advancement of computer technology. And when power was based on information, it would be possible for the multinational companies to overwhelm the nation states to which they supposedly rendered their allegiance.

Still, the Chairman knew that it would always be a question of good against evil, right against wrong. That was simply the way the world operated. It had always been, it would always be so. His dedication to Right was his only religion. He knew, decades ago, that he would have to lead the forces of Good in their last chance for survival. And he would lead with Truth, Truth naked and merciless. That was when and why he had formed MIS. He remained clear-sighted in a world populated by men whose vision was colored by their politics and their petty ambitions.

And he made it his business to clean up the messes made by these shortsighted bureaucrats.

In his rare moments of bitterness it came down to that for the Chairman. ''They're all bureaucrats,'' he said to Sheriff, shaking his head ruefully.

The Chairman had fought wars the public never suspected. He had averted catastrophes of which even heads of state had been ignorant.

His track record, through MIS, was close to perfect. His fees were set accordingly. The money was paid beforehand, in any one of the six recognized world currencies, and there was never any question of showing budgets, or giving refunds. The Chairman did not quibble. A price was set, and it was either paid, or the job was not done.

By the time a client—whether private businessman, European power, or multinational corporation—requested admittance at the electrified gates of MIS, he was in desperate need of the Chairman's services. He was in no position to bargain for a lower rate.

No one imagined, however, that the driving force behind MIS was greed. Rather, The Fort had been built on a solid commitment to the Free World and its institutions. No one knew, really, where the profits of MIS ended up. The Chairman himself, it was rumored, had been born to a family which had been wealthy since before the War of Independence. But there were no inquiries, no stockholders meetings, no battles with the Internal Revenue Service. And the employees of MIS had never been known to make a single complaint in regard to their recompense.

Besides the researchers and the analysts who worked around-the-clock in The Fort, MIS had its outside operatives. How many of them there were, perhaps no one but the Chairman himself knew. They were not a team. Sheriff himself didn't know more than one or two of the others, and that only by sight. The nature of their employment didn't encourage intimacies of any sort.

Yet none of this mattered to Michael Sheriff, really. All that mattered was what the Chairman had said, only once.

"You're my best."

3

MICHAEL SHERIFF LIVED in a pre-Revolutionary farmhouse about three miles farther west of Boston than MIS headquarters. The long, red, rambling structure had survived years of hard use and neglect. He had rescued it from the hands of a large family enthralled with modern furniture and contemporary art.

The first time he had walked into the house he had felt a surge of hardly repressible anger toward the family then occupying it. If he had had less self-control he would have struck the father to the floor. There, in this house that was built in the most honored and loving tradition of the New England farm, blotches of ugly paintings covered the walls. Cheap tile had been laid down over the pegged pine floors. Finely wrought small-paned windows with hand-blown glass had been savaged out, and senseless wide plate-glass picture-windows put in their place. Mercifully the family hadn't had enough money to ransack the place completely.

Sheriff purchased the house on the spot. Even the broker looked surprised at his willingness to meet the asking price. But they were all the more surprised when he named his single condition: The family would have to be out of the place in forty-eight hours. No more. And if not, they wouldn't get the inflated price they were asking for the farmhouse, the barn, the miscellaneous outbuildings, and the sixty acres of pasture and timber surrounding it.

Sheriff could not stand the idea of those disrespectful faddists in that house. The building represented much more to him than simple shelter. It was his own part of this country's heritage. It thrilled him to think that one of the families that had supported this country in its bid for independence had built, lived in, and worked in this very house that now was his. It became his duty—his only duty outside his MIS job—to restore the house to its original state and to give it the respect it deserved. It was, to him, a living museum of the American spirit, a trust that had been bestowed on him by fate.

The family grumbled and tried to get him to reconsider, but Sheriff remained adamant.

"Forty-eight hours," he said.

Two days later Michael Sheriff stood in the living room of the farmhouse and looked around with satisfaction.

He went to the town hall and to the town historical society and investigated the history of the building and the property. Both, he was pleased to discover, had remained intact since 1745. He interviewed the old men who still understood how wooden buildings had been constructed. He read every book on colonial restoration he could find.

And he worked.

The house became the closest thing to a lover that he had had in years. He caressed the wainscoting and the moldings back to life. He restored the original hardware on all the doors and windows. He smashed the plate-glass windows and reconstructed the original windows from a nineteenth-century engraving of the farm he had found in an old history of the town. He scraped the outside walls with patience and delicacy. The house responded to his touch. Its virtue seemed restored.

Even with the help of plumbers, brickmasons, and carpenters, the labor required a full year. During that time he was assigned only the most pressing MIS missions.

The Chairman knew of and approved Sheriff's project. He knew Sheriff had to use his own hands to make contact with the forces and the ideals that he was now defending. The two men silently acknowledged this rebuilding time as the accumulated after-assignment leave Sheriff had always disdained.

The house restored Sheriff's spirit, even as he restored its structure and integrity.

When Michael Sheriff had finished to his satisfaction, he invited a single guest to view his handiwork. It was, of course, the Chairman. After their simple meal of grilled steaks, baked potatoes, and salad, the Chairman and his most trusted warrior walked out into the birch grove that bordered the little stream running through the property.

Birds and small animals scattered at their approach.

The two men saw a small, perfectly scarlet bird fly across their path.

"Ah," said the Chairman, "you have tanagers nesting here. You're very lucky."

"Yes," said Sheriff, "I believe I am."

"Security specialists will be here tomorrow morning," the Chairman said, silently pointing out the nest of the brilliantly scarlet birds. "They'll install the fencing and sensory equipment. And I promise"— he smiled—"they won't ruin the effect you've created. I really could believe, looking around me, that I had been transported back two hundred years." He paused and looked around. "This is a fine refuge, Sheriff. I just want to make sure it doesn't become a trap."

Sheriff nodded assent.

"Also," the Chairman went on, "now that you've finished, I expect you to return to work full time. You've created your masterpiece, but I'm afraid you won't have the time to maintain it. So I've hired a housekeeper for you. She'll take good care of you."

Michael knew this meant that the hired woman would be more than a domestic. She would be able to protect the house, and him as well, if the need arose.

"Also a groundskeeper," said the Chairman. "The woman will be here three days a week, the groundsman four. That should be adequate."

Sheriff didn't protest. He knew the Chairman was right.

* * *

Now Sheriff maneuvered the Volvo up to the security gate at his house. The groundsman was there. The man wordlessly poked at the various buttons on the command console and the metal gates slowly opened to admit Sheriff to his own property. Sheriff didn't even acknowledge the motions that the MIS hired hand had gone through.

Sheriff drove up the long driveway and did get one jab of satisfaction the first moment his renovated house came into view. *Home*, he thought to himself. But the thought hadn't the warmth he had always wanted to invest it with. He had gotten a wonderful feeling during the reconstruction of the house. The labor and the care he'd taken had been important to him—probably they'd been necessary. But now it was done he wondered if he had created for himself a place of refuge or a prison.

The one fact about the house that Sheriff could never ignore for long now overwhelmed him. One truth he could never escape: no one else lived there.

Sheriff parked the car and got out. He walked slowly along the gravel drive, glancing up at the house from several different angles. He'd sanded that wood himself, caressed it the way he caressed women's skin. He'd picked out the simple ornamentation the way some men picked out their cars and their lovers. But now the place looked cold—not like the house of an American revolutionary, but like the house occupied by a Tory general. Stiff and formal. Curtains in the windows, and beds of flowering bulbs, and fragrant smoke billowing from the chimney wouldn't make the place seem warm or welcoming.

Sheriff gathered his few things from the trunk of the Volvo and carried them into the house. Not even the fake housekeeper was there to welcome him. Her name was Katrina and she played her role perfectly. No one would ever guess that she wasn't the recent emigrant from Sweden that she claimed to be. Her chilly attitude toward life, her distant and judgmental manner of carrying out even the most perfunctory conversation had convinced everyone who met her that she was in fact the pious peasant she claimed. In reality, she had been the highest female operative in the Swedish secret service, lured to America by the tripling in wages that the Chairman had offered her. That, and to escape her boredom with the strictly curtailed espionage activities of a socialist Scandinavian nation anxious to remain neutral.

Katrina was not a woman who could accept the idea of working in an office with an underbudgeted staff and orders from ''above'' not to upset the Russians—or the Americans. Working for a neutral country would never satisfy Katrina's lust for life—and, Sheriff thought sometimes, her lust for blood. Three days a week she spent at Sheriff's house, alternating time on duty with the groundsman, but at all other times she was available for short-term assignments for MIS—the bloodier and more dangerous the better.

Sheriff turned on his stereo system—Bang & Olafsson, the best that MIS money could buy. Sheriff liked Beethoven. Meaty music that drowned out thought when a man didn't want to think. One of the symphonies filled the corners of the room, and followed him through the house. He opened windows and let some of the fresh spring air kill the staleness that had built up since he'd gone away.

He took his bags into his bedroom and threw them into the corner. There was no reason to put away any of the clothing. Whatever might still have been cleanly laundered would have been permeated with the stink of the dirty clothes. And there was no telling what sort of small Indian beasts had stowed away in his bags. He hadn't had the best of accommodations. And now he'd let Katrina take care of it.

Sheriff stripped down and added the clothes he was wearing to the pile. He went into the master bathroom and turned on the hot water. The sudden, strong flow from the showerhead sent up an immediate cloud of fog in the enclosed space. Sheriff stepped under it and let the hot water break over his body. He thought at first that he was merely washing away the odor of travel, unstiffening his cramped limbs. But soon he understood he was trying to wash away the memories of the gore he had witnessed, and caused, in India. He had become such an automatic killing machine that it surprised him when he was confronted with these small residues of emotion after the completion of an assignment. But there they were. And no amount of hot water and dewy New England air and clean flannel sheets would cleanse him of the reality of his life. The reality of his work.

He stopped the shower at long last and stepped out to towel himself dry. The music continued to play. The speakers had been placed so that no room was without its outlet for sound—they could convey alarms as well as music. Even here in the bathroom, the strains of the Beethoven were loud and searing. But the music had long since lost its ability to fill the space in the house. After three months, after all the strain and tension of India, Sheriff couldn't feel that he'd actually come home. He tried, as he always did. He dressed in casual clothes and walked slowly through the house, entering every room, opening every door. Noting small changes. Trying, as he always did, to catch Katrina in some small defect of cleaning.

He never did. She was fanatically spotless, as if she had descended from a long line of servingwomen, and had no ambition higher than that of sustaining the home of Michael Sheriff.

The only woman in my house is a passionless robot. Sheriff went to the bar and poured two fingers of Scottish malt whiskey in a short heavy glass. He looked around with some pride at his home and then was struck with thoughts that deadened that pride. He realized that he was viewing this place as if it were a museum, a relict of human habitation—but not the house of a living man. There were no friends who came over and filled these rooms with cigar smoke and the smell of whiskey while they played poker. No woman whose perfumes lingered in odd corners. No children to leave marks on the walls or to make the windows rattle when they ran tramping up the stairs.

Sheriff never questioned his life's choices. Not most of them, anyway. He had signed on with the Chairman and he had, for the past ten years, performed every duty to his fullest. He had fought, he had spied, he had become the best operative in MIS. These things he was proud of. Those and the years that came before: the fighting in Vietnam, the attempt to be a good cop, the hope of becoming a decent man—these were all things Sheriff never regretted.

But the cost?

Realization of the cost did get to him. Especially at moments like this when, after a long and arduous mission, he wanted to come *home*. He wanted to be like another man with pals to go hunting with, a family to gather round him, a woman waiting for *him,* not just lusting after his cock. Goddamn it, he wanted to be able to think about somebody besides himself.

But family men didn't become operatives for MIS. Family men don't commit themselves to a life of fighting for right when the world's going to pot. Family men aren't exposed to the imminent and constant danger of violent death. Family men don't have to plant bombs in their cars, post security guards at their gates, or hire trained assassins as their housekeepers.

He knew there would be food in the kitchen. As always, the utterly efficient Katrina would have stocked the pantry. He felt he should be *happy* to fix a quiet meal at home, to sit in front of a fire with a good bottle of wine, to plan his next purchase for the house. But the loneliness was too great, the weight of this return too onerous. He felt trapped in this house he had rebuilt. Trapped in his aloneness, trapped in the life he had chosen for himself.

He threw back the Scotch in a single swallow, walked out of the house and got back into the Volvo. He didn't want to be there that night, not by himself. Not to think the thoughts he was bound to think, if he remained alone.

4

SHERIFF STOOD in a darkened corner of the bar, disgusted with himself for being there at all. He felt like a shill in a strip joint. But tonight it seemed the only way to get a little female companionship. A little companionship that wouldn't compromise him, that wouldn't obligate him, that would be as intense as his need and as quick as the night.

He knew women in the Boston area. Their names and numbers and addresses were carefully noted in a small book in his hip pocket. On one side of each name were a few words by which he called up a specific memory. On the other side of the name was a list of dates. Like the card at the back of a library book. No woman got taken out more than once a year. That was the rule. More than that, and she started asking questions, angling for a commitment. More than that, and Sheriff began to feel afraid, for himself for growing too attached to one person, and for the lady, whose safety might be compromised by too close an involvement with a dangerous man. Tonight when he had looked through the little book, no one woman presented herself as an obvious choice, so now here he was in the Rainbow Room of the Alpine Inn on Route 128. He wasn't even sure which town it was in. That didn't matter though. All these hotels were alike, all the Rainbow Rooms were alike, all the crowds in them at this time of night were the same.

He wanted a woman tonight, a body to have sex with. He needed a little human warmth, a commodity he himself seemed to be in very short supply of right now. Blood was

human warmth, but he had seen too much of that. You
didn't feel closer to a man just because you'd blown off his
head. Sheriff sipped his second Scotch and looked out for
the woman who'd suit him. She'd be married probably.
She'd be passionate. The women you picked up in bars like
this fell into two groups—those you had to take to dinner beforehand, and those who had only one sort of hunger.

The Rainbow Room was a meat market. It was ironic that
practically the whole damn menu was steaks. It was one of
those places where everybody drank hard liquor, and lots of
it. And where everybody came from someplace else. As
likely to find a woman in there from Seattle as Sudbury. The
music was too loud, but maybe not, because who wanted to
talk, really? People nodded in time with the songs on the
jukebox, and smiled at each other when the lyrics were sug-
gestive.

Sheriff got picked out before he had done any choosing
himself. The woman came up to him, obviously drunk. He
could smell the bourbon on her breath. She was drinking it
on the rocks, as quickly as if it were a diet drink. She stared
at Sheriff lewdly, in a way that reminded him of the whores
of Amsterdam. She unabashedly rubbed her crotch against
his hip as she sidled past him to the bar, letting him feel the
mound that she was so obviously offering him.

She was attractive. Small, perhaps five-three, with the
carefully made-up face and perfectly coiffed hair of a
woman making it in business. He imagined her spending her
days fighting against the entrenched bureaucracy of some
enormous, impersonal corporation. She'd have to make it
impossible for them not to advance her through the ranks. At
the workplace she did everything possible to erase her femi-
ninity and deny her womanness. Now, in the security of the
Rainbow Room, she was swinging in the opposite direction,
about as far as she could go.

So he wasn't shocked or surprised when her hand coyly
dropped down and brushed his crotch. Her face showed her
disappointment when she realized that he was giving no indication of a positive response. The flesh beneath his trou-

sers was impressive, but still flaccid. For some reason, she just wasn't right. Or he wasn't.

"What's a girl to do?" she murmured.

"Keep on hunting." Sheriff smiled back.

She walked away from him, not surprised that he hadn't responded, only momentarily disappointed. He saw her as she presented herself in a similar manner to another man, farther down the bar, and after a while, she moved to an unoccupied table and seated herself with an expectant smile. Sheriff realized that this woman was quite possibly making two, three times the salary of most of the men in this place. She could be five times smarter than the rest of them put together. But at night, in the Rainbow Room, her spirits and her self-image as watered down as her bourbon, she was reverting to the most helpless image of womankind she could think of, just to secure the same kind of companionship that Sheriff was looking for himself.

The world was fucked-up.

He waited another drink and a half hour more. It was a slow night in the Rainbow Room, though at first it had seemed crowded to him. The women were taken, or coy beyond his interest in talking them out of the coyness. The disgust he felt being in the Rainbow Room finally overcame his horniness. He hated being part of the sideshow. He put down his glass, not even finishing his drink, and walked out of the bar.

When Sheriff got to the parking lot he heard a scuffle over in a far, dark corner of the space, in the shadow of one of the blind motel walls. Human bodies, in some kind of combat. Sheriff froze in his tracks briefly to wonder what could be going on: a brawl between drunken friends? A mugging? A rape?

He moved quietly toward the sounds, lifting his head sharply at a sudden, sharp wail. A woman's voice in inarticulate protest.

A rape.

Sheriff crouched and moved even more quickly. His training directed him toward the sounds by a route through the shadows, between parked cars, along the brick wall. He stopped short, hidden behind a bush, where he was within a few feet of the action.

His eyes had already adjusted to the dark. He could make out four figures. One much smaller than the rest—a woman. The other three were men at least his own size. They stood over her, forming an arc that forced her back against the blank brick wall of the motel. Their feet sank silently in the redwood-chip flower bed. Then Sheriff caught the momentary gleam of a sodium light on metal. A knife.

"Come on, bitch," Sheriff heard one of the men growl. "You might as well put out and save us some trouble. 'Cause you *are* gonna put out."

The other two men laughed obscenely. The woman was bent over, trying to protect herself. One of the men grabbed her arms, and pushed them wide apart. Sheriff saw that her dress had been ripped open from the neck down to her waist. Her exposed skin and bra shone sickly white in this dark protected area. She made some protesting sound, and Sheriff realized suddenly that this was the woman who had approached him in the bar.

The same hands that had taken away her arms now reached up and pulled hard on the bra, forcing the white fabric up, loosening her full breasts to view. Several hands shot out and fondled her naked nipples. "Noooo . . ." she groaned in protest against the harsh touches.

"Oh yes," said the only man who was talking. His hands moved down and lifted up her skirt. Again there was white skin, and again a flash of white fabric as her panties were exposed. Sheriff heard the sheer cloth rip, and a moment later he saw the black triangle between her legs. "Oh yes . . ." the man repeated as his hands worked on her sex, his middle finger bringing another sharp protest as it disappeared into her. She was obviously dry and not ready for the invasion.

Sheriff looked at the scene in disgust. The woman had only wanted to barter some companionship for the evening. She had only wanted to negotiate—one on one—a break in her solitude. He understood all that. She had wanted no more than he had. She certainly hadn't done anything to justify this violation.

Sheriff heard a zipper undone. The leader's pants dropped to the ground, and now it was his briefs that trapped the light. "Got a great present for you, Sarah, yeah, a great present."

He took her hand and placed it on the extended flesh that was still trapped in his shorts. She jerked away as if it had been burning hot metal. He slapped her hard across the face. "Cunt! You've been begging for a piece of cock in there all night. Okay, you got one here. You got three here. So get down on your knees and thank us for it. And you know what to do when you get down there . . ."

The other two men forced her down. The leader had reached into his briefs and liberated his erection. It seemed a tiny spear aimed at Sarah's head.

Sheriff's movements were so fast that the three men hadn't any chance to prepare themselves. He leaped across the small space between them with more speed than they could have prepared themselves against, even had they known he was there and intending to come at them. Without breaking his stride Sheriff lifted his left foot and sent it flying into the exposed crotch of the leader. The soft hairy skin of his testicles disappeared under the fierce blow of Sheriff's shoe. A scream of agony filled the air. The leader's body collapsed into a fetal position with such animal response that he nearly trapped the invading foot before Sheriff could retract it.

The other two now had their turn to react. Each man had a knife. Switchblades. Strange for suburbanites, Sheriff thought, and automatically he began to reevaluate the situation. To give room for a little more possible response on the part of his adversaries.

The knives flashed toward Sheriff. The two men had obviously fought together before; those knives weren't alien in their hands. Their movements had the unconscious coordination of men who had been in combat together. They'd probably raped together before, as well.

Sheriff's hand, kept in shadow by his own body, shot out toward the man on the left. He connected with the wrist that held the knife. The bones broke; Sheriff noted the sound with satisfaction. He didn't have to hear the knife falling, because the knife wouldn't be any good anymore. But he did hear it just the same: metal slipping through the branches of a small bush.

Sheriff turned toward the one man remaining upright. There was a glint in the eye of this third man. Not of fear. He was sure of himself. He welcomed Sheriff's intrusion. He was going to have more fun with Sheriff than he would have had with Sarah. That's what the glint in those eyes said. The man didn't pay any attention to his friends, both of whom were groaning, squirming in the redwood chips of the flower bed at this blind end of the Alpine Inn. Their pain meant nothing to him except an excuse to kill. If he needed one.

He was still that cocky when Sheriff leaped forward and smashed his head against the brick wall. Another cracked bone. Skull bone. As though drunk, the third man slid down the wall at a slow, slow pace, his battered head listing slowly side to side.

Sheriff grabbed Sarah's arm and pulled her out of the shadows. Her dress was ruined, her bare breasts remained exposed to the late night air. In the distance, a drunken couple stumbled out of the bar, laughing. Snuffling, still drunk, Sarah tried aimlessly to cover herself. Sheriff took her arm and guided her toward his Volvo. He opened the door for her and pushed her inside.

When he got into the driver's seat, he said once, very distinctly, "Give me directions for your home."

She swallowed hard, but something in the quality of his voice told her that this man didn't want to hear anything else.

"North on 128," she stammered.

Sheriff turned on the ignition, and in another moment they were off. In his rearview mirror, Sheriff saw one of the men he'd wounded stagger out into the light. His blood looked black in the harsh light of the sodium-arc lamp.

Sheriff followed Sarah's directions to an apartment complex in Lexington. He knew about it. It was the most expensive in the area. Luxury condominiums that appealed to the young professional class that worked in the companies along Route 128. He suspected his first impression of Sarah was right. This woman had to earn a great deal of money to live here.

He stopped in front of the door she indicated. He stared straight ahead through the windshield and waited for her to get out. The drive, though, had given Sarah just enough time to understand what had happened. The one fact that took priority over the rest was that this man had saved her life, beaten her attackers, and punished the would-be rapists in a manner most women would like to see their rapists punished—with sickening violence. In her muddled mind, Sheriff was her hero now. "Won't you come up?"

The question was put tentatively. Her hand came over and touched Sheriff's shoulder. He looked at her and said, "No." But his answer wasn't unkind. It was matter-of-fact. He had no need of reward for what he'd done.

Sarah climbed out of the Volvo and again tried to readjust her clothing without success. Sheriff looked at her and thought that he *should* have some response to this woman and to the sight of her naked nipples, now erect in the cool evening breeze. But he couldn't find it. Sarah looked at him sadly. "Thank you," she said, probably realizing that since all the words in the world would have been inadequate, the simplest were the best.

Sheriff nodded in response. That's all. She walked into her building while he sat in the driver's seat and watched her, a final bit of protection to make sure that there wasn't some last danger to her this night.

Then he drove away.

On his way home Sheriff realized he was invigorated by the fight. It had broken his boredom. But what did that say about his life? That on the first night back, after three

months in India, after more fights than most professional
soldiers would bludgeon their way through in a lifetime, he
had to go out and join a street brawl to feel good.

He thought, too, about Sarah. It hadn't been her intoxica-
tion or her forwardness that had turned him off, not by a
long shot. It had been her naked need, the indication that she
would want more than a one-night stand with a decent stud.
After the fight that need had only grown in her. There would
have been no way that Sheriff could have fucked her and
walked away after a morning cup of coffee on opposite sides
of a dinette table. She would have wanted more.

She would have wanted as much as Sheriff himself
wanted.

He should have hired a whore that night, a woman who
knew what she was giving, and could put a price on it in dollars. If a whore has needs, you don't hear about them.

At least, he thought, working the security console at the
gate, at least I'm tired enough to get a good night's sleep.
The excitement of rescuing Sarah had accomplished one
thing: it had rid him of his jet lag.

One final thought occurred to him that night as he
dropped between the sheets alone. That he had probably
killed one of the men back at the Alpine Inn. The one whose
testicles were crushed. Or the one whose head had been
smashed against the wall. So what kind of total did that give
him? Michael Sheriff didn't know how many men and
women he'd killed. And right now he couldn't even remember what year he'd lost count.

5

SHERIFF WOKE the next morning to the sounds of domestic work. A dull, faraway noise was the engine of a vacuum cleaner. He looked over at the clock. It was only 7:30 in the morning, but Katrina was already at it.

He sprawled out on his bed and tensed all his muscles, sending waves of blood into the inactive areas, pumping adrenaline through his system. He relaxed back onto the mattress and listened to Katrina clean. What, he wondered, was behind that woman? Two years after her arrival and he still didn't understand. Her three days at the house every week were part of a cover, but she had thrown herself into that cover. She was the perfect Swedish housemaid. She looked the part, dressed the part, acted the part in town when she went to do shopping.

But the rest of Katrina's life was spent in the bowels of MIS. Her job there was to analyze the vast amounts of information on Soviet and East Bloc troop movements. She didn't have to live out this secondary role in Sheriff's house. But she did, to the limit. And occasionally, for a reward, she was given a special assignment. Sent back to Scandinavia for a few days, or down to Washington, where she did things that few housekeepers do. She killed people. Katrina was one of three MIS assassins.

Sheriff stood. He quickly showered and shaved and dressed in sharp-creased slacks and a cotton polo shirt. He put on socks and slipped his feet into highly polished loafers. The condition of his clothes and the sheen on his shoes were all part of Katrina's handiwork. Sheriff would have kept everything with equal military precision, and that fact allowed him to appreciate Katrina's competency to the degree he did.

When he came downstairs he was greeted with the smell of food. A big breakfast. He could discern sausage and some kind of bread—probably pancakes. There were sizzling eggs and when he got to the dining room table he knew that the waiting glass of orange juice was freshly squeezed.

The *Boston Globe*, The *Wall Street Journal*, and the *New York Times* were all in place, waiting for him. He sat down and opened the *Globe*. He became immediately absorbed in an amusing story about the strange change in the political fortunes of a radical Indian group. The pontificating columnist had created an entire scenario about the fall of the group, how they had lost their base in the population, what had happened to their funding. None of it had anything to do with reality.

What had happened to the organization was simple. Michael Sheriff had destroyed it.

Katrina entered with a steaming platter of food and a freshly brewed pot of coffee. She automatically poured some into his cup. "Good morning." She said the words as though she had performed the same actions every day for the past ten years. No hint that Sheriff had been absent for three months.

He reciprocated with a noncommittal "Good morning," and continued with the *Globe*.

As he read, a familiar and somewhat painful thought went through his mind. Whatever Katrina was, and whoever Katrina was, she was also a spy. She was spying on him. He assumed—and was sure he was correct—that she reported any change, however slight, in his manners, his actions, or his possessions to the Chairman. This surveillance was part of her function. Katrina marked the limit of the Chairman's trust in Michael Sheriff.

Sheriff's home was a fortress. He was both its defender and its prisoner. The armed guards who patrolled it were in the employ of someone else. The electronic equipment was trained on him as well as on any possible intruders. His privacy and his possessions were shams.

The thought chilled him. He put down his newspaper and looked out at the yard. He wondered if the tanagers the Chairman admired had returned. They nested in a red sugar maple.

Katrina came back into the dining room. She stood over him and stared down with disapproval as she saw the full plate not yet touched. My mother wasn't such a bitch about this stuff, Sheriff thought. Katrina broke her gaze and finally handed Sheriff a written message. She went back into the kitchen without having spoken a word.

Sheriff instinctively knew what the message was. He opened it and found his speculation correct. It was a single letter: *C*. The Chairman wanted him.

A half hour later, Sheriff entered The Fort. His face was known and his fingerprints gave him entrance. He strode down the blank corridors past dozens of closed and locked and unnumbered doors. His khaki trousers and open-collared shirt set him apart from the conservatively dressed persons he occasionally passed in the hallway.

He presented himself silently, at parade rest, in the ante-chamber of the Chairman's office.

His secretary said simply, "You're expected."

Any other man, even the head of a major government, would have had to wait while she announced him. Michael Sheriff merely nodded an acknowledgment, walked over to the mahogany doors, and went inside.

The Chairman was seated behind his desk—a large and exquisitely beautiful Chippendale, a museum piece. In matching chairs before the desk sat two men. One of them Sheriff recognized immediately—an ex-astronaut who, since the emasculation of America's space program, had become spokesman for the world's largest aerospace firm. Sheriff disliked him instinctively. The second man was an African, tall and proud, very much at ease in his native dress. He looked at Sheriff carefully, and Sheriff gazed back. Each man acknowledged in that look the forthright manhood of the other.

The ex-astronaut scowled. The African at last smiled warmly.

"This, gentlemen," said the Chairman, "is Michael Sheriff, The Shield."

6

THE TWO OTHER visitors rose. The former astronaut—Sheriff remembered that his name was Jack Flank—was closer and Sheriff shook his hand with mechanical disinterest. Flank was a media freak; the kind of male who measured his self-worth by the number of national television anchormen he calls by their first names. He was a turkey so far as Sheriff was concerned. Someone whose fame rested on his ability to pull the right levers in a space capsule.

But the other man sent out all the messages that Sheriff did admire. The tall black wore a brightly colored dashiki. He carried his body with obvious pride and confidence. The marks on his face were the permanent evidence of his tribe's adolescent rites of passage. They signed him forever as one who had earned the right to carry the title: Man. Their handshake lasted a little longer than necessary, as though they were sealing a pact, not simply meeting one another in the offices of a third party.

"You know Mr. Flank, of course," the Chairman said from behind his desk. "This is Prince Motala, the Leikawan ambassador to the United Nations."

"Good to meet you," Sheriff said brusquely, nodding to both men. The African prince didn't return the verbal gesture, but continued to study Sheriff.

Flank was the one who spoke next: "Mr. Chairman, while my company is perfectly well aware of the abilities and the record of MIS, I really do think that it's a bit much to expect us to pay these exorbitant fees for the services of just one man." Flank shot a disapproving glance toward Sheriff.

"I think, Mr. Flank, we should discuss this with Mr. Sheriff before we make any quick judgments," Prince Motala said, betraying the fact that *he* had just made such a quick judgment: in favor of Michael Sheriff.

"Gentlemen, why don't you all have a seat." The three of them followed the Chairman's suggestion. "Michael"— the older man turned and looked at Sheriff as he spoke— "Mr. Flank and Prince Motala have approached MIS with a matter of great concern and urgency." That statement was unnecessary. *Everyone* approached MIS in that way.

"The prince's country, one of the fairly recently independent states of Africa, is in a position to aid the United States and her allies greatly. Geologists have recently discovered, in the northern regions of Leikawa, vast deposits of two different ores, both of which are in great demand in the West.

"These two ores are also, by strange chance, also the source of a fair percentage of the Soviet Union's hard currency. However little of these elements we have, the Russians have them in great abundance. Since the Russians control the world markets in these two minerals, we are not only forced to pay high prices for them, we are also dependent upon our enemy for that supply. Obviously, an unsatisfactory situation.

"The ores," the Chairman concluded with a sense of drama that was habitual to him, "the ores are cobalt and uranium."

"The Russians don't control the uranium market," said Sheriff. "I understand that the United States has a fairly plentiful supply."

"That's right," said the Chairman. "We have enough for ourselves. But our allies? Great Britain, France, West Germany? They have no internal source of uranium, and must buy where they can. But cobalt is the more pressing issue. Cobalt is necessary for the manufacture of certain alloys used in our most sophisticated aircraft. And when I say necessary, I do not exaggerate. Without cobalt, the damn things wouldn't get off the ground."

"That's where Intercontinental Mining and Industries comes in." Flank spoke up quickly, as if his presence as representative of a company was more important than that of the ambassador of a foreign state. "Our needs for cobalt are skyrocketing. If we can get to the Leikawa reserves, now that we know how extensive they are, we'll be guaranteed our supplies for the foreseeable future."

Sheriff ignored Flank. If the point had been put in terms of America's strategic concerns, he might have had more interest, but Sheriff had had enough to do with multinationals to know that they only cared about their returns on investment, their profits, and the prices of their stock. The multinationals did not usually concern themselves with what effect their enterprises had on the American economy and well-being. Instead of responding to Flank, Sheriff turned to the prince. "What does all this mean to you?" The prince began to speak immediately, as if he too were ignoring the presence and words of Flank and had only been waiting to converse with Sheriff.

"Leikawa is a poor country, poor beyond the comprehension of most Americans. Our economy has been strangled by incompetent bureaucrats and greedy provincial rulers. Liberation from our colonial masters hasn't brought prosperity, it's meant only devastation and decay.

"Our concern—my concern—is that these recent mineral discoveries have a chance of bringing Leikawa out of its misery. The potential wealth in these ores is comparable to that the Arabs enjoy with their petroleum.

"That of course is a very positive perception. There's a less encouraging one. The sale of these minerals is going to be an enticing prize for some of our people. Especially those government officials who already sense that they will earn enormous fortunes from this natural wealth. It appears that the Russians and their friends have already understood that. There is too much money and there are too many new arms converging in the less patriotic areas of Leikawa, if I may so call them.''

Ignoring the Chairman's disapproving scowl, Sheriff lighted a Sobranie. He used the cigarette smoke to hide behind, just for a moment. He wanted to process some of the information these men were throwing out at him.

"Then,'' Sheriff said after a moment, ''Flank's only here because the Russians got to Leikawa first. If he'd had his chance you might still be at MIS, but asking for our help against him rather than with him.''

The prince looked at the ex-astronaut and smiled. ''You are exactly right, of course. Mr. Flank's presence is one of his convenience. It only so happens that his convenience matches the legitimate national interests of Leikawa.''

Sheriff nodded. He trusted his instincts. They had told him that the prince was someone he would admire, grow to like and respect. They also told him that Flank was an asshole. He had just wanted to clear up the reason for the men's joint appearance on the other side of the Chairman's desk.

Flank, though, wasn't at all pleased with this attack. ''Now wait a minute! Intercontinental Mining and Industries is a true American firm. We pride ourselves on our American heritage, on our—''

''Is that why you've moved almost all your primary industrial plants to Latin American and East Asia?'' The Chairman spoke with offhanded contempt. ''So that Americans would lose their jobs and your operations could be left out in the open in unstable countries at the mercy of every terrorist group that can get up the cost of ten sticks of dynamite and an alarm clock? Or is that the reason you refuse to hire Jews in your Arab plants and Arabs in your Israeli operations? Are all those examples of your commitment to the American way?

''Perhaps more in line was your bungling attempt to assassinate one of the only true democratic leaders in South America, an operation so poorly conceived and executed that it led directly to the rise of a military dictatorship.

American way, indeed!'' The Chairman ended his quick, cutting speech with a snort.

"That military dictatorship is the most stable government in the southern hemisphere,'' Flank objected.

"Stable because of the ruthless policies of constant terror and dehumanization. Stable because the populace is frozen in horror at the capricious and diabolical methods of suppression used by your 'friends.' ''

Flank, red in the face and holding on to the arms of his chair, looked about to speak, but the Chairman held up a warning hand. He wasn't finished.

"We know why you're here, Mr. Flank,'' said the Chairman. "Don't think that our willingness to entertain your proposal comes out of any admiration for Intercontinental Mining and Industries. We know full well about your policy of calculated cost overruns that help to ensure that the federal budget is constantly strained to meet your projected profits.

"You're only here because if we can get your firm to give Leikawa a decent contract for its mineral reserves we can have a hand in helping to establish a *really* stable democratic regime in that part of the world.''

"That, and because we'll pay your highwayman's fees,'' Flank shot back.

"If you choose not to pay our firm's fee, you can leave, Mr. Flank. *Now!*'' Only Michael Sheriff had expected the loud order that was accompanied by the Chairman's fist slamming on his desk. Both Flank and the prince seemed shocked. "MIS will gladly broker a mining agreement between Leikawa and another firm willing to cover our expenses.''

The threat wasn't idle. Flank evidently understood that. He glanced at the phone on the Chairman's desk and seemed to realize that there wasn't a single corporation in the Free World that wasn't accessible to MIS at a moment's notice. If Intercontinental Mining and Industries didn't want to play by MIS rules, they didn't have to. Plenty of others would. Flank obviously wasn't going to risk testing that little bit of conventional wisdom. He sank back into his chair and tried to hide his annoyance at being treated in this brusque, straightforward manner. Didn't they know he had been an astronaut, and deserved at least the semblance of respect? Didn't they know he was a hero?

What the Chairman and Michael Sheriff did know was that a man of Flank's limited ability would never have risen to his corporate heights if it hadn't been for the fluke that allowed him a moment of glory—a moment that was really the result of chance and coincidence, and was by no means a proof of his exalted manliness or capabilities.

The media and its consumers might have assumed that Flank's role in the space program was a result of an intensive constitution and a grueling struggle by which he proved that he was the best man, the one with the right ingredients and the best stuff. The truth, which the Chairman knew since he had just finished reading the files on the astronaut, was that Flank had been chosen for a single reason—his extraordinary malleability.

That a man with any kind of flight experience could captain a spacecraft had long ago been an accepted fact. What that man might do once he had caught the public eye was a much greater variable. The American space program had devised a series of craft that could be flown by a novice with diarrhea. After that they had to make sure that the novice was as easily manipulated on the ground as the capsule was in space.

They didn't want anyone who would misuse the public exposure by supporting unpopular causes. They didn't want to create a hero who might afterward—at any time in the course of his entire life—cause the government embarrassment. So the criteria on who would fly into space was quite simple. Was the man so unimaginative that he wouldn't ever even consider the possibility of an extramarital affair? Was he so brainwashed that he would never think of leaving the middle-American way of life? Would he, in short, be content to follow the government manual on the conduct of heroes for the rest of his life? They wanted no one who'd suddenly get religion, or who'd shoot his wife, or who'd lend his name to gambling casinos, or run for political office.

Flank had been perfect. Dull to an unspeakable extreme, lacking the ability to form an original thought, unable to lead, so lackluster that any prolonged exposure to him was guaranteed to elicit contempt. He actually thought he had made a wise move by trading in his experiences for a six-figure income at Intercontinental Mining and Industries when he retired from the air force. The NASA officials who had chosen him were shocked as well—shocked that he had been so foolish to take half of what he might have gotten. He had proved even more leaden than their projections.

"What's going on in Leikawa that makes this all so difficult?" Sheriff asked Prince Motala.

The black man seemed saddened by the question. "Leikawa is in the hands of a corrupt regime. I suppose I should be grateful the regime is as incompetent as it is—at least those in power are not capable of putting into practice the repressions Mr. Chairman has just spoken of . . ."

Flank shifted uncomfortably in his chair.

"The government's largest problem is its inability to control the diverse factions of Leikawa, mainly tribal groups. There are some sections of our population that prefer to ignore the advantages of civilization. They are being allowed to move about unchecked, and their savagery is dragging the rest of Leikawa down with them.

"Our hope—at the moment—resides in one person: the chieftain of the Fashanti. A noble man in the old traditions, he speaks to all our people with great moral authority. His sole interest is in the advancement of all the peoples of Leikawa. Many know that. He is our only hope for a unified and progressive regime.

"If we could secure him a place as the head of state of Leikawa, then—and only then—could we work with the potential riches of our minerals and change things. We need his presence. With it, we could guarantee that our minerals would be sold at fair market value to Intercontinental Mining and Industries. This is what we offer on our side."

Sheriff considered: "What you need me for is to bring down the military and prepare the way for this man?"

Flank snickered. The presumption of this man! Of the Chairman!

But Prince Motala evidently took Sheriff seriously, for he said, "We need you to do much more than that. The military would fall easily. We need you to protect the miners who are already there, and we need you to mobilize the most significant of our progressive tribes, the Fashanti. Nothing can be done unless you can accomplish that."

"And you are yourself Fashanti?" Sheriff asked.

"No, not at all," the prince replied. "I am from one of the most minor tribes. That is the only reason I am ambassador to the United Nations, because my appointment to such a prestigious post wouldn't offend any of the more powerful groups. Nor is the man who must come to power in Leikawa in any way related or allied to me and my people. He is the king of the Fashanti. That would normally mean he could never rule the whole country. But it is a measure of his position and his trust in the minds of our people that he can overcome that prejudice."

"Why doesn't he just do it, then? Why doesn't he just lead a revolution himself?" Sheriff asked.

The prince smiled sadly again. "The king of the Fashanti is a spiritual man. Like Ghandi, his idol, he refuses to take part in violent revolution. He insists that his moral superiority will bring about good in Leikawa itself. He will not even lead his own tribe into battle, but watches placidly while their fighting spirit disintegrates.

"Given the leadership of government, without having to do anything to secure it, he will be a good leader. There is no doubt about that. But until then, the matter is in our hands."

Sheriff puffed on his Sobranie and looked over at the Chairman. They had come up against too many such leaders in their careers together. Men—and women—who would avoid the bloodstains necessary to protect their peoples' rights, leaders who would retreat into spiritual isolation rather than face the need to fight against the violent elements in the world.

The prince would obviously be the man behind the throne in Leikawa if all this was brought off. Sheriff knew that. He instinctively understood that the prince would be the kind of man who merely wanted to see good done. His payment would come from the knowledge that his people would be protected—that they might even prosper. He was the opposite of a man like Flank. The prince would gladly give up the spotlight, so long as his goals were accomplished.

"A revolution." Sheriff said the word simply, starkly. He crushed out the cigarette. "That's what we want?" He glanced first at Prince Motala, then at the Chairman.

The Chairman paused only a moment before replying. "A handing over of power, the elimination of certain foreign elements in Leikawa. Revolution? It's a word to frighten the naive." All that meant: yes.

The Chairman turned to the two visitors. "The contracts are prepared. Management Information Services is ready to accept this assignment. You both know the terms."

Flank glared at Michael Sheriff. "Just one man. I'd feel a lot better—"

"One man backed by all the resources of MIS," the Chairman interrupted coldly. "One man will be quite sufficient." The Chairman punched a button on his desk and his ever-efficient secretary walked in, carrying all the necessary documents.

7

THE BUZZER SOUNDED. Sheriff went and answered the intercom that connected his house and the guardpost. "Yes."

"He's here."

The intercom went dead. Sheriff went over and stood in front of the fireplace. He watched the flames flicker and listened to the crackling of the dry wood as it burned. "He"—of course—was the Chairman. Sheriff had long ago accepted the way the Chairman disregarded any privacy Michael might have wanted for himself. He could appear at Sheriff's gate and be admitted without Sheriff's permission. The fact the guard even notified him was a courtesy for which Sheriff should probably be grateful. His job, his life, were unlike other men's.

He kept staring at the fire, thinking of that, even when the front door opened. Not bothering with even the superficial politeness of a knock before entering, the Chairman simply walked in and took a seat in the big wing chair that faced the hearth.

"Have you examined the material?"

Sheriff didn't answer immediately. After a couple of beats, he finally turned. "Couldn't you at least go through a little 'Hello, how are you?' At least wonder if I had a headache, or wanted a drink, or needed some time off?"

The Chairman studied Michael with a quizzical stare. After a moment, he asked, "Why? You're in peak health. If you weren't, I'd know about it. As to social pleasantries:

they're used with people who choose to be social with one another. I assumed we were far beyond that.''

Sheriff didn't answer. He looked back to the fire.

''But perhaps I should have seen that something was wrong. What is it?''

''It might have something to do with being home for less than twenty-four hours after a three-month assignment when I'm told what's next on the agenda. It might have something to do with coming back to a house where the servants were spying on me as if I were just waiting for an opportunity to spill everything I ever heard to the Russians. It might have something to do with always being alone.''

''Ah.'' The Chairman seemed to understand everything at once. ''I suppose it is a fault of mine that I have grown to expect you to be beyond these adolescent concerns of the middle-class male. But why should you be concerned about being spied upon? We're all under observation to one degree or another. You simply happen to know where the cameras are located. You've done nothing in ten years that you'd be ashamed to see in your file—nothing that I can think of off-hand. Your life has been beyond reproach, though I can't say I entirely sympathize with your taste in the opposite sex. And there was a time you took a kind of delight in laying waste to all Katrina's efforts at surveillance.

''As to the assignment, you must know that I don't have any control over timing. Problems crop up around the world without any regard to my personal convenience. Besides, you're not expected to leave on the next plane. You'll have a week to ten days in which to prepare yourself. I'm quite surprised to hear you speak this way, in fact. You've always been anxious to be in the field. Except for the period when you were working on the house, you seemed to dislike staying put. I would have thought you'd be pleased for the opportunity of helping a man like Prince Motala.''

Sheriff still said nothing.

''And there was something else, wasn't there?'' mused the Chairman, looking about the room. ''Ah yes, loneliness.'' Michael turned and glared—the topic wasn't a safe one. "Well," said the Chairman easily, "there was a time in your life when you were not alone. It was your decision to abandon that situation. I don't think you have a right to blame me for the consequence of those actions."

"I had no choice," said Sheriff. The words sounded weak, even in his own ears.

"I'm not sure about that," the Chairman said mercilessly. "At any rate, if there were options, you chose not to investigate them. What you might have done—"

"Stop it!" Sheriff's face and voice were adamant now. "Leave it alone. I'm fine. Let's get to work."

He walked over and took the seat closest to the Chairman. In front of them on a low table were two stacks of documents. Sheriff began to sift through them. This material was the typical background package that came from MIS whenever he was to start an operation. Stacks of computer printouts gave more information on Leikawa's economic and political situation than either the US or the UN could have provided. Cassette tapes contained sections of speeches by the most important public figures in the country. The Chairman considered mere transcripts inadequate. Hundreds and hundreds of slides, taped on videocassettes, recorded the countryside of Leikawa, its architecture, the various tribes that made up the country's population. Films showed native dances, the festivities surrounding the emancipation several years before, and even some grainy, surreptitious clips of a torture session in one of the provincial prisons. A notebook held nearly a hundred maps showing all aspects of the geography, climate, vegetation, and industry of Leikawa; and bound in more notebooks were satellite photographs of the whole country, as well as startlingly detailed photographs of the northern region where the cobalt and uranium had been discovered.

Every once in a while Sheriff would come across a piece of data that still carried the impressive TOP SECRET FOR YOUR EYES ONLY stamp across the top page. He had long ago stopped wondering whose eyes were being referred to or how the Chairman got his hands on such things. Sheriff had heard plenty of rumors about the Chairman's connections. There was talk that he had a member of the joint chiefs of staff on his information payroll and even more speculation on how many members of congress were in the casual employ of MIS. There were a fair number of people around who would have turned over documents to the Chairman with no compensation at all, so great was their faith in the ultimate patriotism of Management Information Services. The head of the CIA might be co-opted on occasion, but never the Chairman. But to Sheriff none of that really mattered, so long as the information he needed was always the best available. Whenever he went into the field for MIS, Sheriff knew that no one had more background information than he did. Information, he knew, was as much a weapon as fifteen hand grenades strung round his waist on a belt. As the recipient of the information gathered by MIS, Michael Sheriff was the best-armed warrior on the battlefield.

Not that the best information always provided the best news, however. It was clear to Sheriff as he went through the data that Leikawa was in trouble.

The forests of Leikawa were the dark side of Africa. Not only were they the stalking grounds of some of the most exotic and dangerous beasts on the continent, they were also the hereditary home of the Kindu, the most-feared people in that quadrant of the world.

The Kindu had apparently learned nothing at all during a hundred years of colonial rule. They had accepted Christianity to the extent of the goods they received from the missionaries. When the missionaries went away, the Kindu burned their crosses for kindling, and reverted to their age-old savagery. Law and peace had no meaning for the tribe. They understood only Power. It was the only ideal the Kindu acknowledged.

The Kindu conquered when they could, and scavenged when they could not. Whereas the Fashanti learned from the Europeans everything that would press them a little further along on the road to civilization, the Kindu desired only the most base sort of profiteering.

For the whole of their history the Kindu had been a self-indulgent tribe. When food supplies were low they raided the nearest village, whether that village belonged to another tribe, or was merely another Kindu settlement. When their own women died off through neglect or maltreatment, the Kindu ensnared and raped those of the Fashanti. What little work the Kindu settlements required was performed by those the Kindu had enslaved.

Only one event had ever really affected the Kindu: the arrival, almost two centuries before, of an Arab slave trader. The Arab offered gold in exchange for healthy human flesh.

From that moment the Kindu gained a purpose. They literally corralled countless black men, women, and children and sold them over into a destiny of servitude, horror, and violent death. The Kindu were not prejudiced. They would sell members of any tribe not strong enough to withstand their raids. And they sold to any merchant who would buy—Portuguese, British, French, Persian, and American traders alike made their way to the forests of Leikawa and emerged with their long, miserable train of naked, shackled Africans.

The Kindu were furious when the declining slave trade eventually ended. What were they expected to do? Farm like the Fashanti? The new colonial masters, who were scarcely less mercenary than the slave traders, stepped forward with a solution. They gave the Kindu rifles and snappy uniforms. "You're soldiers, policemen!" they were told.

The Kindu were pleased. Things did not change so much after all.

The line of trees that stood phalanxlike to face the savannah provided the only natural border in this part of Africa. The demarcation never showed on political maps, but all the inhabitants of that portion of the continent were deeply aware of its significance. It was the boundary between the two major tribes of the young republic of Leikawa.

The savannah belonged to the Fashanti, a peaceable people who had roamed the plains from time immemorial. In the past few centuries they had developed systematic agricultural techniques. Having eagerly learned all they could from their alien and mostly ineffectual colonial masters, they had solidified those first steps toward an efficient economy and life-style. They were no longer passively dependent on the whimsy of climate and an invariable animal migration. Owing purely to this progress, the Fashanti had tripled their number in the past half-century.

The Fashanti had held firm to their native ideals of justice and honor and had used the colonial courts to institutionalize those ideals. They had always been one of the prideful examples benevolent Europeans would point to when they spoke of the hope of the new Africa.

Until ten years ago.

The sheer numbers of the Fashanti and their own considerable skill as warriors had kept them from suffering the worst depredations of the Kindu. But the appearance of uniformed Kindu armed with rifles and the colonial masters' authority altered the entire situation. The Fashanti felt themselves mortally endangered. Only constant pressure on the administration kept the Kindu in check.

Then, ten years ago, the whole protective structure crashed apart. Yielding to global politics, the colonialists abruptly abandoned Leikawa. A leader for the new black government was chosen from a tribe that inhabited neither the forest nor the savannah but the coast, where the capital was located. The Kindu, however, kept their uniforms and their rifles.

In that brief decade the Kindu reign of terror destroyed the Fashanti's history-long march toward civilization. The Kindu extorted triple taxes from the Fashanti, surreptitiously burned outlying Fashanti villages, and slaughtered Fashanti children and women of childbearing age. They laid waste to all the seats of local government and justice, and established their own ferociously cruel and arbitrary system of punishment.

The economy of Leikawa was about to collapse completely. There was only one hope against that eventuality: the discovery of an enormous deposit of cobalt and uranium in an isolated stretch of barren land north of the savannahs, but belonging—by old treaties—to the Fashanti.

"It's not a pretty picture," Sheriff said after he had read through most of the material.

The Chairman scowled. "It's a typical example of the European legacy in Africa. They were only anxious to secure their trading rights, and to foster their own impression of imperial glory. The colonies they created utterly ignored the realities of native African politics. The Europeans severed tribes in two and three portions with artificial boundaries. They lumped sworn enemies into the same political divisions. It's been like the partitioning of Poland—but on a continental scale.

"It was bad enough when the Europeans were there, when they were themselves dealing with the colonial divisions. It's become impossible now that self-governing nations exist with those artificial boundaries. Putting the Fashanti and the Kindu in the same nation guarantees a civil war every ten years for Leikawa. National unity is a joke in Africa. The Europeans have left behind whole peoples to die at the hands of their own governments.

"Look at Nigeria. A completely nonsensical state. Part Islamic, part Christian, part native religion. Three groups of sworn religious enemies expected not only to coexist, but create a nation unified in spirit and purpose. Ludicrous!

"The real crime is the way that the truly noble people of Africa must suffer. The Fashanti are one of the best examples I know. Under a thoughtful dispensation, they would have been given their own sovereign country. Their natural intelligence, their will to succeed, and their intrinsically positive worldview would have allowed them to create a truly successful state, a model for the rest of Africa. The Kindu, on the other hand—" He broke off abruptly. "I'm going to need a cognac on this one," the Chairman said suddenly, shifting in his chair.

Sheriff went and poured two snifters of his best Armagnac. Only when he had brought them back and the Chairman had warmed the dark amber liquid in his hands, did the older man continue.

"The Kindu are the worst kind of conservative. They are focused on one thing: the continuance of their life as it is. They would destroy anything that would disrupt it. Their *life* though is something very precarious, indeed, in the face of advancing modernity.

"Slavery in its basest form is a part of Kindu culture—if I may call it that. We know that slavery exists in parts of Leikawa, and so does the government. But no one moves against it. Like so many other things, if it's not seen, then no one feels a need to deal with the issue. The simple form of Kindu slavery—enforced labor, no wages, sexual privileges for the masters, and physical torture as a method of encouragement as well as punishment—seem surreal to those who read the *New York Times* and the *Boston Globe*. No one can believe that such things exist today. Though it's a common enough thing, even in parts of the United States.

"If the cobalt is mined on an extensive basis, the systematic slavery of the Kindu will come into the spotlight. If Leikawa is suddenly so wealthy and so important, then there will be journalists, tourists, visiting officials from other countries. All those groups avoid Leikawa now. But in their presence, the Kindu would be seen as the nearly subhuman people they are.

"The Kindu do not intend to allow that to happen.

"More: without funds, the Leikawan government not only doesn't threaten the Kindu, they are dependent upon them. The Kindu long ago became the police and local militia for the European colonists. They were always willing to fight anyone for any reason so long as the fighting produced money and blood. If the Kindu have any ethic at all, it's based on those elements—money and blood.

"The Kindu could destroy the Leikawan government at

will. But it serves the tribe's purpose to have the world focus on the capital rather than the interior. But if that government suddenly became wealthy, ah! then it could arm and deploy troops of its own. Then the Kindu would become vulnerable to real defeat.''

Michael boiled down the Chairman's analysis: "So the Kindu, who could make a bundle in their own way from the ores, are willing to forgo that just to maintain their current power. They see themselves as pretty big fish right now, and they just want to make sure their pond stays the same size.''

"They also have to make certain that the Fashanti don't take control of the government. By keeping Leikawa in a state of near collapse, with only a semblance of civilization, they assure themselves a tyrant's power over poverty-stricken slaves. In the past ten years, the Kindu have wiped out two small tribes in the northeastern quadrant of the country. Utterly wiped them out. If there were a genocide event in the Olympics, the Kindu would walk away with all the medals.''

"Anybody supporting the Kindu?" Sheriff asked.

"The Russians," the Chairman said without hesitation. "Though they're not putting their hands on directly. They've fielded squads of Czechs this time. Supposedly traders, but we know they're actually arming and training the Kindu. Like training a swarm of wasps how to sting with greater efficiency . . .''

Sheriff swirled the Armagnac thoughtfully.

"We have to move quickly," said the Chairman. "We have to help the Fashanti counterattack before the Kindu become utterly dominant in the country. We have to mobilize the Fashanti and make sure they can stand by themselves afterward, as the guardians of a free Leikawa. It's not sufficient to stop the Kindu. Simply to cut off their supplies and defuse the Czech menace won't stabilize Leikawa. It will only postpone the arrival of the country's doom.''

Sheriff sipped the cognac. "So I'm not just going in there to destroy an enemy, I'm supposed to create a nation as well. I'm not only going to take on a well-armed tribe of African slavers, I'm supposed to instill another tribe with sufficient pride and determination to turn themselves into the beacon of freedom for a whole continent.''

"You've had more difficult assignments," the Chairman said. "Now, shall we look at some of these tapes? You can see the Kindu in all their savage glory."

. . . 8

THE FILM that had been transferred onto the videocassette
was black-and-white, grainy, and silent. The camera had
either been hidden, or it had been operated by an amateur. It
wasn't immediately clear whether the recording of the
atrocities had been made by someone anxious to have the
horrible truth verified, or by someone else who had done it
merely for a kind of insane pleasure with the Kindu bestial-
ity. Sheriff also couldn't imagine how Management Information Services had gotten hold of it.

The film was pornographic. There was no other word for
what Sheriff witnessed on his video monitor. Over and over
he played the tape, speeding it up, slowing it down, advancing it frame by frame—always hoping that he could detect
some visual prevarication, some piece of editing, something
that would allow him to think that the reality had not been as
bad as what he saw on tape.

But he couldn't. He was left with the conviction that what
he had seen was real.

The tape began with a map inserted by MIS, pinpointing
the location of the action: a cobalt mine in the north of
Leikawa.

Then the film began. Innocently. Almost like a little trav-
elog.

A mountain in the background, and in the foreground, a
small cluster of buildings, obviously constructed to house
and feed the workers in the mine. The little village seemed a

strange intrusion in that remote portion of Africa. Tiny flower beds had been planted in front of the wood-frame houses, and the little homes themselves bore touches of domesticity: painted doors, curtains in the windows, children's toys on the shaded porches.

But a moment later that quiet panorama was changed.

A black warrior—KINDU flashed on the screen, as a kind of subtitle—*ran out of one of the houses, clutching a pile of clothing to his bare chest. A dog ran out after him yapping, but a moment later the dog dropped dead.* Shot by someone standing out of camera range, Sheriff surmised. *A few moments after that, two windows in the house exploded inward with more shots. A shadow of a falling body slanted past the broken window.*

There was something extraordinarily unpleasant about this silent footage, to Sheriff. The step-by-step destruction. The film blinked black and then came up suddenly on another scene.

Two screaming white women. One of them already naked, the other having her clothes ripped off her by two grinning Kindu warriors. The women were roughly handled, prodded in the sex, slapped hard across their breasts. They were then tied up in a coffle of several other naked women.

An abrupt cut to:

Two houses, back to back, on fire. Two snarling dogs chained to the front porch of one of the burning structures. Ten dead men lying faceup in a row in the front yard. Each had been shot through the head, and the earth was stained dark with their blood. Two small children ran up, pointing and opening their mouths wide in silent screaming.

Another cut to:

A woman lying on the ground, her skirt thrown up over her head. Absolutely still, she might have been dazed or dead. One of the Kindu had mounted her and was making exaggerated thrusts inside her. Two more Kindu warriors stood beside him, uncovered, ready to take their turns. They held up their guns and shook them.

Sheriff had seen rapes before, and he had killed rapists.

He had watched young children weeping over the corpses of their slaughtered parents. He had seen houses and villages burned to the ground. Cruelty wasn't confined to the Kindu. But what came next Michael Sheriff had not seen.

In a clear space, the children had been gathered together, guarded by a single warrior. With a sharp-pointed spear the guard prodded the children who tried to unhuddle—leaving little black puncture marks of blood in their skin. In the background cowered a half dozen women and two men— evidently all that remained alive of the inhabitants of the mining village.

Even at such a distance, Sheriff could make out the terror in their faces.

Several Kindu warriors approached the adults. They were carrying fair-sized timbers, of the sort used to shore up mining excavations. These were thrown onto the ground between the parents and their children.

The film cut forward in time:

The timbers were arranged in a kind of pyramid or teepee-like structure. One timber for each of eleven adults. Already the two men and three of the women had been set with their backs against the foot-wide timbers, their feet bound with rope, their arms raised above their heads. And their crossed hands nailed to the wood with metal spikes. Long trails of blackish blood seeped from those new wounds, snaking down the captives' arms, splashing into their upturned faces, puddling on the ground. Two more women were dragged forward, their feet tied and their arms raised above them. Then their hands were nailed to the timbers.

Sheriff had never seen a real crucifixion. He wondered if it got worse.

It did.

The film cut to:

The pyramid with all eleven adults staked. The children at this point had been herded into the center of the pyramid, and encircled with a single rope that was pulled tight and staked to the ground. Two of the children were limp, unconscious or dead, held upright simply because the rope and the proximity of the others did not allow them to fall. The others were crying, and reaching out toward the adults on all sides of them. The children looked wet, glistening, as if drenched by a brief downpour—but there was something sticky-looking about the liquid that covered them.

Because it was gasoline.

Two Kindu, with five-gallon cans, were sloshing on more gasoline. On the parents' genitals and legs.

"Oh shit," Sheriff said aloud.

Then a white man suddenly appeared. With matches.

At first Sheriff thought he was one of the miners, but when he saw the box of kitchen matches in his hand, he changed his mind. Sheriff stopped the tape, ran it back, stopped the action, and studied the man's face. Memorizing it. Then he reluctantly allowed the tape to run forward.

The white man struck one of the matches and tossed it toward the exposed genitals of one of the surviving men. The gasoline-saturated flesh and hair burst into bright white flame. The victim opened his mouth in a scream of agony— Sheriff could hear it in his brain.

—and then one by one each of the adult victims was similarly ignited. When each was burning and screaming, the white man took one final match, struck it and then dropped it back into the box. The box he tossed toward the group of roped children in the middle of the burning pyramid. It caught fire in midair and then dropped in their midst. The knot of children caught fire in one small, intense explosion of flame.

The pyramid burned so brightly that the film was overexposed. In a sea of shivering whiteness, Sheriff now and then saw contorted faces, and burned limbs, and scraps of dead flesh that belonged to the victims of the Kindu.

THE NEXT FEW DAYS Sheriff spent reading and studying all the information that MIS had provided. He viewed the tapes—especially those of the Kindu atrocities—over and over. Katrina, who apparently had been informed concerning the impending assignment, had even begun to cook food for him that approximated the diet of the Fashanti and the Kindu. In this manner, over the past few years, Sheriff had sampled not a few of the world's minor cuisines. In this case, Sheriff wasn't certain that he'd ever develop a real relish for monkey's brains or lion *osso buco*.

With the work came a welcome and expected relief. His mind was completely focused on Leikawa, on his mission. So long as he kept at it with his usual unswerving determination, Michael Sheriff didn't have to think about other things.

He didn't notice, for instance, the emptiness of the house or how clean the rooms were, and remained, even at those times Katrina was away. The furniture, the walls, the floors all maintained a kind of polish that spoke louder than anything else that he was the sole inhabitant. Cabinets and closets and shelves were empty. Sheriff wasn't a collector or an accumulator. Nothing showed his personal taste. Even the pictures on the walls were merely those presented to him by the Chairman over the years. He liked them—but they weren't really his. Sheriff had one rack of record albums—all the music he liked, it seemed—and these he played over and over again. He had a small library, but it mostly contained reference books. He sometimes read for pleasure, but then he tossed the books out, knowing he wouldn't read them again. Whenever he thought about the spareness, the emptiness of his life, he got depressed. At those times, he poured a glass of good whiskey straight, sat in a chair that faced a blank wall, and thought about the choices he'd made in life.

His passion was for adventure. His lust was for the field. His loyalties were to MIS and to the Chairman. His vocation was the good of the world. So long as he could tick off these four items, and say to himself truthfully that they were still true, he forced himself to rest satisfied. Few men in this world could say as much. Knowing that he was true to himself and his ideals helped console Michael for the gripping emptiness of his existence.

But even the Michael Sheriffs of the world can't control all the variables of existence. Even The Shield couldn't prepare himself against *every* eventuality.

Sheriff didn't know it, but Saturday was to be the most challenging day of his life. For the first time in ten years, he would be forced to relinquish control of his own destiny.

Early that morning the groundsman called from the gate and announced simply, "Visitor, sir."

"Who is it?" Sheriff asked, surprised, wondering who could have been let through. But the groundsman had already rung off.

Sheriff stood in the front door, waiting.

He assumed it was the Chairman; he couldn't imagine that the groundsman would have let anyone else through.

It wasn't the Chairman's BMW. It was an older, inexpensive car that came up the long gravel driveway.

When Sheriff caught sight of the Nevada license plate, he grew uneasy.

There was a man inside the car. Sheriff couldn't tell any more than that.

Sheriff felt damp sweat gathering beneath his clothing.

He had expected this visit someday. He had hoped it would never happen. It *shouldn't* happen, he always told himself. And he had always known that it would.

When the car was directly in front of the house, it slowed to a grinding stop on the loose gravel.

"What will he look like?" Michael wondered.

The door of the car opened and a very young man stood out. He put his forearm on the roof of the car, and looked over it steadily, into Michael Sheriff's face. The two men faced one another with steady, but not angry, expressions. Their shoulders were set squarely, but the stance was natural, not challenging.

"Roger," said Michael, in quiet acknowledgment.

"Dad."

"Come inside," said Sheriff.

The boy walked around the car and allowed Michael's right arm to wrap around his shoulders. Silently, father and son went into the house. Michael pointed out the couch to his son. He took a leather chair in the corner of the room. They were close enough to talk comfortably, not so close they had to touch.

Michael saw his son through a time warp. Roger was himself twenty years ago. There was the boy he had once been.

In Michael Sheriff, Roger saw the man he would become.

The teenager looked a couple of years older than his actual age because of the bushy brown moustache that covered his upper lip. He had already reached Michael's six-foot height. He might possibly grow an inch or two taller yet. His shoulders were broad and strong, the chest expanded and slightly exaggerated by hard exercise. He wore only a white T-shirt, jeans, and scuffed boots. The clothing displayed long and strenuous wear.

Roger could look at his father and see the man he would become. The same muscular strength was there, slightly more rounded and mellowed by thirty-eight years of age, but just as obviously potent as his own. There was Roger's own face with slight scars and the weathering that was the result of two decades of personal warfare carried out in a whole array of climes. The hair, only slightly thinning, was the same brown hue as Roger's, but sprinkled with gray.

They studied one another and through both their minds rang a single refrain: *This man has my blood in his veins.*

"Why are you here?" Michael Sheriff asked his son at last.

"I've come to live with my father."

The words cut. Deeper than the Kindu knives. This was his son. And he could not let him stay.

"No," said Michael, with every appearance of impassivity. "You can't stay with me."

Roger said nothing.

"Why did you leave your mother?" asked Michael, and very nearly choked on the words.

"Mother is a whore," Roger said simply.

Without reflection, in pure blood instinct, Michael Sheriff rose from his chair, took three steps forward, and slapped his son across his face.

Roger's head snapped back, and the print of his father's hand rose bright and red on his shaven cheek.

"Don't *ever* say that to me," Michael Sheriff said coldly.

Roger did not apologize. He had spoken only the truth. And he knew that Michael Sheriff knew it was the truth. Roger, going through what he had gone through in the past ten years, would not retract the judgment he had spoken on the woman who had given him birth.

Trembling still, Michael Sheriff sat down again.

"I turned eighteen three days ago," said Roger. The words were a little garbled, for his jaw still trembled with the violence of his father's blow. "And three days ago, I packed up and drove off."

"And came here," said Michael. "How did you find me? How did you find this place?"

"I was sent directions," said Roger.

Michael Sheriff considered this with astonishment.

"Were you *told* to come here?"

"No," said Roger. "I was simply sent directions. I came of my own free will."

"How did you get past the man at the gate? What did you say to him?"

"Nothing," said Roger. "He seemed to be expecting me."

Michael Sheriff didn't dare allow himself to hope. All these years of enforced loneliness, all these years that had passed in which he had not allowed himself to tell his real name to a single person he came across. Here was his son, whom he had not seen in over ten years. It nearly stifled him every time he thought that he had given up his only son to *that woman* who was the boy's mother. And here Roger was, before him, at first glance appearing to be everything he would have wanted in his boy. He thought it would kill him to send Roger away, but he was steeling himself to do just that.

Sheriff would have to send the boy away, and without telling him the reason—just as Michael had left the boy and his mother eleven years before, without giving any reason at all.

If Roger knew even that Michael Sheriff was a part of the secret world of MIS, the boy would be in danger. And if the rest of that secret world ever found out that this was his son, it would only be a matter of time before Roger was taken hostage, or simply dispatched.

But Michael also knew that this young man deserved to understand something about his father. He had a right to know why his father had remained so distant, why he had—except for the occasional Christmas or birthday card—remained such a fleeting character in his life. If for no other reason, Michael had to talk to Roger because Roger was truly the most important person in his life.

Roger could never know about the times when the very idea of him had allowed Michael to hold on, when it had seemed so much easier just to slip away. The struggles Michael had endured when any other man would have surrendered. Whenever the danger was too great, the torture too effective, the goal too obscure, Michael Sheriff had only to think of his son.

His son was the reason for all of it.

AFRICAN ASSIGNMENT 69

And Roger could never be told how much his father loved him.

"Do you want a beer?" Sheriff asked.

Roger nodded. "I drove straight in from Washington today. Eight hours. And I've been sleeping in the back seat of the car."

Sheriff got up and brought two cold cans of beer from the kitchen. He handed one to Roger and watched the young man open the flip top and take a long sip. Michael did the same with a surge of pride at this first beer shared by father and son. There are little symbols in life that can turn out to be not so little after all; this was one. Michael Sheriff couldn't allow himself to hope that he and Roger would share any others.

But as they shared their small ritual, Sheriff thought about the Chairman's part in all this.

Had the Chairman seen that ultimately Michael would be unable to deal with his loneliness? Sheriff looked at his son. *His son.* The thought assaulted his head. Why else had the Chairman played this, his trump card? Did he fear for Sheriff's loyalty? Or his sanity? Did the Chairman look on the boy as a kind of hostage?

Such thoughts were useless. Sheriff had never been able to decipher the Chairman's actions. But if the older man had sensed that the deep longing for family and companionship in Sheriff was a need that had to be fulfilled, then perhaps—only perhaps—there was a way to prolong this unlooked-for reunion.

The thought stunned Sheriff. To live with his son? To know that someone in his own image slept in an adjoining room? To know the presence of his own blood in the house he had rebuilt? To possess some reason for going on, besides MIS and his patriotism?

To live without hope is ultimately tolerable. A man can go through life understanding that he will always be alone. But for such a man to taste real companionship and then have it snatched away would be to suffer the ultimate cruelty, harsher than death itself. Could Sheriff really risk this?

Could he really allow himself to savor the presence of his son and then survive if Roger were taken away from him again?

For the first time in years, Michael Sheriff felt fear.

. . . 10

Michael Sheriff opened his eyes. Morning. Usually it was a purely mechanical time of day for him. Get up. Shower. Walk to the dining room. Read the papers and the briefing files that were delivered nearly every morning. The remainder of the day was hardly less exactingly programmed. The daily exercises. A midday meal. More reading. More exercise. Dinner, usually alone. At night there might be a woman.

Sheriff's days had been the same for the last ten years. Except for the time he was in the field, his life consisted of this constant preparation of his mind and body for the next assignment. Sex existed as a method for relieving tension. Romance was nonexistent. His companionship was limited to Katrina, the guard at the gate, and on rare occasions the Chairman. Even at that, he might pass an entire day without really speaking a word aloud.

This morning was different. It was so different he wondered if it weren't a dream. For the first time in his memory he waked with a sense of happy anticipation.

He got out of the covers and went over to his bureau. He pulled out a jock and running shorts. He pulled on track shoes over woolen socks. The scratchiness of the fabric convinced him he was awake, not dreaming. He relished that sensation.

He walked out of his room into the long second-floor corridor. He paused for several moments at the closed door nearest his own, on the same side of the hallway. How do I do this? he wondered. On the other side of the door was his son. Asleep in his room. Do you knock to announce your entry? Does an eighteen-year-old have the right to that kind of privacy? Or do you just walk in and assume he's asleep? Sheriff was paralyzed for a moment. There was so much he didn't know about being a father. *Well, what would I do if he was just a buddy? I'd go right on in.*

Sheriff pushed open the door with uncharacteristic tentativeness. The room was flooded with morning light. Roger was sprawled across the double bed. His head lolled to one side, his mouth hung open in the relaxation of sleep, and an arm hung over the side of the bed. He seemed, even in sleep, to be savoring the luxury of a double-width mattress.

Sheriff walked over and gently shook his son's shoulder.

Roger's eyes jumped open. There was a momentary expression of confusion. *Where am I?*

Sheriff realized then that this was the first night his son had slept under this Massachusetts roof. He put his hand back on Roger's shoulder. The boy relaxed, smiled and stretched, lifting his body up off the bed with a leonine exertion. Only when he collapsed back did he speak. "Morning."

"Hi," Sheriff replied, uncomfortable with the laconic response. "I, uh, I run every morning. Thought you might be interested. If you'd rather stay in bed, I can come and get you for breakfast later . . ."

"No, no, that's great. Give me a sec, I'll get ready."

"I'll wait for you in the living room," Sheriff said, attempting to give Roger more privacy. The boy obviously didn't feel the need for it. He was already out of bed and striding naked over to his knapsack which had been left on a chair in the corner.

"This is great. I've been doing a lot of running, but recently, well, I just lost it. If you run every day, I'll get back into it." Roger was pulling on his own athletic gear.

Michael was looking out the window. *Running together every day . . .*

"All set," Roger announced. Michael wondered if it was an act for him. If it was he'd have to tell the kid that it wasn't necessary. He didn't want to push this whole setup. He didn't want the boy to think that he had to do everything Sheriff did.

But Roger was already out of the room. Michael followed him. In the warm spring morning they walked outdoors and wordlessly Roger began to do limbering exercises. He did them so intently and so competently that it was immediately apparent to Sheriff that this was no act. Roger did run regularly. The father fell in beside his son and started his own warmup.

When they had stretched and twisted their muscles into looseness in preparation for the run, Roger asked, "You have a regular course?"

"Yes. It's all inside the compound."

The boy looked puzzled.

Roger had no way of knowing that he was living inside a secure fortress. "I'll explain all that later," said Sheriff. "But yes, there's a course. I measured it out. Five miles."

Michael Sheriff nodded and began to move down the driveway. The morning run was a part of his life so accustomed and internalized that the track was like the drive a commuter makes to his office every working day. Sheriff realized that it would have been impossible to describe the exact sequence of tree trunks, patches of uneven ground, shrubs, and ditches by which his course was minutely plotted.

He followed his own track, paying conscious attention to it for the first time in years. Here he knew he left the driveway and moved onto a well-worn path in the woods. He wouldn't have been able to tell anyone else that he knew to take the turn because of the oak sapling that listed at a precise forty-five-degree angle. Nor would he have remembered the precise stone at which he invariably planted his left foot when leaping across a small tumbling stream—but because Roger was directly behind him, Sheriff saw that purple stone as if for the first time.

Michael Sheriff had walked through the last few years with so little passion that he had forgotten the assault on the senses that this trail could produce. There was a particularly astonishing vista, overlooking the rolling meadows to the west. He hadn't paid attention to it in recent memory, but now he interrupted his stride to point it out, wanting to make sure Roger saw it. He smelled the pine of the forests for the first time in ages and hoped the boy appreciated the odors as much as he had himself the first time he had explored this section of his property.

He was used to the solitary pounding of his heart as the five-mile track drew to an end, but now he was astonished at the sound of his son's labored breathing beside him. He smelled the boy's sweat nearly as strongly as his own. His arms were moving with someone else's as he ran. His most solitary activity, his time of particular reclusiveness, was being spent in the company of another person. He was matched stride for stride, breath for breath, by a male of his own blood.

My son.

They came to the house and both stopped at the same moment, bent over, panting in deep drafts of oxygen to their lungs. Sheriff glanced at his son. Roger's face was blotched with effort—it was evident that he wasn't used to five miles a day. Sheriff suddenly felt a surge of responsibility overcome him. This wasn't just his own little exercise anymore. He stood straight up and although his chest ached for more relaxation, he assumed a pose that was supposed to be nonchalant. His arms crossed over his chest, his face in repose, he waited while Roger kept up the attempts to overcome the effects of the exercise. Sheriff felt he had to give Roger something to work against.

Sheriff studied the boy's stamina and prowess. *He's in good shape.* Roger weighed considerably less than Sheriff. He'd need to build up some weight. Maybe Sheriff could get the boy some protein supplements. It would probably be a good idea to have him work out regularly on a set of weights as well. Increase his bulk. The shoulders could be widened, the chest could stand some expansion. But all in all, Roger wasn't a bad specimen of an eighteen-year-old.

He'd have plenty of opportunities to improve here in Massachusetts. "Ready for a shower?" Roger asked Sheriff. The father nodded. The two walked into the house and toward their rooms. "Two for breakfast, Katrina," Sheriff yelled into the kitchen as they passed. Sheriff knew the housekeeper would have already begun preparations. He just liked the sound of the words.

In the shower Michael Sheriff found his mind and his emotions continuing their strange, unfamiliar patterns. *What did the kid like to eat?* Remembering how little time the boy's mother had spent in cooking, Sheriff thought it likely that Roger had eaten nothing but junk food since he was eight. There was no junk food at Sheriff's house. Food built the body. Roger might just have to learn how to eat as well. Katrina would see to that.

As Sheriff towelled himself dry, he wondered what Roger would want to do over the next few days. Had he ever been East before? Was Nevada the limit of his experience? Maybe they should go into Boston, take in a really good restaurant. Had Roger ever been to a play? Would he want to? What was on stage in town now?

Did Roger have any money? Was that car insured? Were the tires safe? Maybe Sheriff should just go out and get him a new car. And drive down to New York to try it out. Was there time before Sheriff had to go to Leikawa?

Leikawa! Shit! Why now? Why did he have to go just when Roger had arrived? What if he didn't come back from Africa?

Sheriff froze. His body went icy cold. He caught his face's reflection in the bathroom mirror. That thought hadn't bothered him in years. *What if he didn't come back?*

Roger had existed in Sheriff's mind all the time they had been separated, but only as an abstraction, Michael realized now. Roger would be secure enough if anything happened to Sheriff. There were insurance policies, a trust fund for college, the deed to this land and house. The *items* of inheritance were his, they always had been. Sheriff's conscience had been assuaged by the efforts of the Chairman's lawyers.

But in the last few hours, Roger had become concrete, and very real. His son had slept under his roof, raced with him, drunk beer with him. Sheriff could even hear the running water through the bathroom wall as his son cleaned up. Now Michael Sheriff had to face the fact that he had someone here in his house. His *home.* Someone who would be waiting for him to return from Africa. Not a hired spy posing as housekeeper. Not an employer who took everything—even Sheriff's safety—for granted. Not a piece of ass panting for his cock.

His son was going to be waiting for him.

What if he didn't come back?

Sheriff dressed in casual clothes, combed his hair, and went down to the dining room. He sat at his usual place and stared with only bare comprehension at the place setting that had been laid across from his. A plate, silverware, a juice glass filled with orange liquid, a larger glass of milk. A coffee cup, as yet unfilled. *Does he drink coffee?*

Sheriff was pouring his own cup when Roger came in. The young man walked with a bouncing step. Cleanliness and freshness breathed out of every pore of his body.

Michael Sheriff looked up into the newly scraped face across from him. *Old enough to shave.* But Roger's short-sleeved shirt showed forearms and the lower half of his biceps covered with only the finest blond fuzz. *He'll grow hair there like mine.* Then Sheriff was amazed at the details he found himself noticing about the boy. How strange, those things that he'd never thought about. A son. You'd think about his schoolwork or his athletics or how many friends he had—not whether he had hair on his body. Maybe you'd even think about his girl friends and wonder . . .

"About time you got some decent clothes," Michael

Sheriff said sharply. He immediately wanted to kick himself. What an asshole thing to say. Here's a kid sitting at his father's table for the first time in ten years and Sheriff had to lead off with a reprimand about his wardrobe.

Roger didn't look up. An expression of subtle defeat spread across his face. It was enough to make Sheriff doubly angry with himself. "Sorry, don't know why I said that." It was difficult to get those words out. His first apology to the boy. Was it good to apologize?

"Nah, it's okay. I guess I do need some stuff."

The words weren't spoken with much conviction. Sheriff tried to make the best of a bad situation. "Look, we can go into Boston. Really do you up."

"Okay." It must have worked at least a little. Roger looked up at his father and the beginning of a smile worked across his lips.

"What else would you like to do?"

Roger poured himself a cup of coffee. *He does drink it.* "I don't know." The boy seemed puzzled. "Are you taking off work to be with me?"

"No," said Sheriff, started to add something, then didn't.

"Are you rich? Don't you have to work or something? I don't even know what you do."

Oh, I kill terrorists, assassinate dictators, foment revolutions, and act as bodyguards to heads of state. How the hell was he supposed to answer a question like that? "Well, like I said, we can go into Boston. I usually work out in the afternoon. You could join me then, when we come back. If you want to."

Roger paused a moment. He knew his question hadn't been answered. "Sure," he said after a moment. "We can work out together. That'd be great."

Sheriff felt the distance between them. He'd put it there. The boy was trying. And the part of Sheriff that belonged to MIS and the Chairman was holding back.

Had to hold back.

Katrina came out with a platter of waffles and a boat of hot Maine maple syrup.

How is a professional killer supposed to work this father shit anyway?

11

THE FASHANTI HEADMAN stood in mortal agony, not from the pain, but from the disgrace. His hands were bound together and then fastened to a tall pole high above his head. He was naked. His totem necklace, the mark of his viceroy status in the tribe, had been ripped off and broken in the dirt.

In front of him the Kindu continued their rape and pillage, their murder and enslavement. The headman was full of disgust at himself and his people that this had occurred.

He was an old man. Well beyond eighty years, he had lived through nearly a century of Leikawa's history. He had learned well from the European missionaries, he could read and write. But even with those gifts he now thought that he had learned his lessons at the mission school *too* well. The white religious men had emasculated his soul. They had led him into a peaceful life, encouraging agriculture and thrift, piety and virtue.

It seemed to the headman that his current state was the inevitable result of listening to all those white skins with their fine words. The words had sounded good. Milk and honey and long life and fat babies and happy wives. There had been immediate rewards, too, tools from the government, seeds from the missionaries, and eventually, independence for Leikawa. Noble sentiments, all that.

But in the end, the headman now knew that the real effect of the missionaries' work had been to leave the Fashanti defenseless in the face of their blood enemies. The Fashanti men were unable to hold weapons, the women were like cat-

tle whose only fate was to be slaughtered, the children left
without any notion of the dark and bestial side of African
tribal life. White Jesus couldn't see through the black smoke
of burning Fashanti villages.

The Kindu were so contemptuous of the Fashanti and
their peaceful ways that they now dared to bring even their
own children along on these raids. The headman remembered well what Fashanti life had been like before the missionaries had done their worst. He remembered how all this
part of Africa had quivered with fear at the sound of the
Fashanti war horns. Their wail, out of a non-Christian black
hell, had formed terror in the hearts of their enemies—even
the Kindu.

The Fashanti had been the most stable and prosperous
tribe in this part of the continent. Their adherence to basic
concepts of justice and human dignity had made this one of
the most peaceful and happy quarters of Africa. But now?
Now they were farmers who prayed to a god that condemned
war, no matter how or why that war was fought. A god that
insisted submission was a virtue, and that weapons were
made with Satan's scaly hands. With the collapse of their
ability to fight and defend the things they held important, the
Fashanti had prepared the way for the Kindu depredations.

The headman saw it all now. He saw it all too late.

The only thing that amazed him now was the presence of
white men with the Kindu. Three of them, strangely colored. Not like the missionaries, whose white skin had
toasted and darkened eventually. But with burned red skin
that showed they hadn't been long in Africa. One was
scarred. Another grinned and drank from a flask. The third
stood still with his arms crossed, and now and then craned
his neck for a better view of some atrocity against the headman's people.

It was this third man—perhaps the leader of the white
men—who seemed most interested in the way the Kindu operated. He was speaking to one of the Kindu who was
dressed in western clothes, speaking in a language the Fashanti headman didn't understand. But one thing the headman

did comprehend. The white man was a dangerous enemy, who could look at the burning huts, and kick away the screaming bleeding children, and turn a deaf ear on the screams of the violated women as he noted the technicalities of Kindu warfare.

The scarred white man just stood there grinning. With obvious satisfaction. The fires seemed to excite him. He laughed at the naked squirming women. A man who killed for pleasure. Murdered for sport. Like the Kindu themselves.

It was this third white man who filled the headman with loathing and fear. Because this third man had moved slowly about the circle of burning huts to stand near a group of young girl children—in fact, one of the Kindu seemed to be rounding up the children for him. They stood weeping before him, but did not dare move—this third man wielded a casual knife in his hand, and flicked it against the black skin of any child that attempted to stir. The Fashanti headman saw the bulge in the white man's trousers, and was disgusted by this debaucher of children.

So, the missionaries had done their job and he had helped them. But those years hadn't erased what had come before. Now the war cries of the Fashanti sounded in the old man's head. He prayed, not to the white god that ordered submission, but to the Fashanti god that demanded vengeance. He prayed that some of the Fashanti skills had been passed down to men young enough to fight. Prayed that the Fashanti here—those dead, those dying, those raped, persecuted, and enslaved—would be avenged. He wanted the retribution to be as cruel as what he now saw in front of him.

His thoughts were interrupted by the sudden appearance of a half dozen Kindu children. Boys, just boys, but already they had the bloodlust of Kindu warriors twice their age. They—like their fathers—were drawn to the sight of a defenseless foe. The old man tied to a post was just what they needed to cut their teeth of savage Kindu masculinity.

They taunted him. He, insistent on some shred of dignity, refused to acknowledge their taunts. They had long, thin

sticks in their hands. They began to switch him with them.
The cutting blows burned at his thighs, his manhood, his
stomach. But if this was to be the headman's last hour on
earth, it was to be time spent as a Fashanti warrior, not as a
sniveling slave. He clenched his jaw, tightened his body, allowed no sound to escape from him. He would show the god
of the mercenaries what it was to withstand pain and forgo
any sign of submission.

The boys were angered that their game elicited so little response. They had just come from using the same switches
on a line of teenaged Fashanti girls who had shrieked most
pleasingly when they had first tasted the reality of Kindu
slavery. But this old man would not react. The boys were in-
creasingly frustrated, and finally grew somewhat frightened
of the stoic figure in front of them.

One boy in particular decided that the old man must be
broken, taught who were masters here. The resisting slave
must be given a lesson before he died. The boy moved
closer. The headman watched him. The Fashanti war cries
had grown clearer in his head. Moves, tactics, strategies, all
came back to him now. He would die with self-respect.
Now he knew it.

The Kindu boy was close enough. The old man called on
every particle of strength left in his dying body. Muscles
tensed and limbs tightened and the boy suddenly let out a cry
of pain. The headman's legs had not been tied—the Kindu
had thought him too old and feeble to have use for them. But
now they were wrapped tightly about the Kindu boy's neck,
squeezing hard and gagging the adolescent murderer. The
other boys were frozen in terror. They had never seen anyone resist the Kindu. Now there was one of their own, his
face bulging with trapped blood, his eyes popping from their
sockets, his arms flailing in panic.

Finally one of the boys began beating at the Fashanti
headman's legs with his switch, and all the other boys followed suit. But the old man was going to die anyway, he
knew. He wasn't going to let go because of some cuts on his
legs. He took pleasure in the death of this boy. One Kindu

who wouldn't grow up a murderer to savage another Fashanti village. He felt the boy's life grow weaker, but that only made him squeeze harder. He thanked the ancient Fashanti gods, and then he smiled at the Kindu warriors who at last appeared, drawn by the cries of the children.

The boy caught between his legs was dead. The headman allowed him to drop to the ground. Two Kindu warriors, with anger and frustration on their faces, raised rifles to his head. He didn't care. He would die a Fashanti warrior. They couldn't take that away from him.

His last prayer was that there would be other Fashanti warriors. Younger ones, stronger ones.

He only heard the beginning of the rifle fire, and then he was dead. The noise of the shots echoed in ears that would not hear again.

12

BIG SAM'S was a restaurant in the middle of Boston's South End. Not that part of the neighborhood redone and prettied up by relocating suburbanites. But the area near the border with Roxbury where Boston's blacks had been ghettoized for decades. The buildings here were decrepit. The elegance of their architectural lines was often lost behind aluminum-siding walls. The first floors were often obscured by crassly commercial facades like that constructed for Big Sam's.

Whatever it looked like, Big Sam's had the best fried chicken and the meatiest ribs in the city. Jimmy Carter ate there during his presidential campaign, and a night later there was a fatal shooting in the men's room. It was that kind of restaurant—and it was Michael Sheriff's favorite place in Boston. The warm greeting he got from the waitresses and the cook made it obvious he came there often.

Father and son took a booth along the back wall. Michael ordered for Roger. A chicken-and-ribs barbecue platter, slaw, and corn bread. Two beers. The waitress Michael had introduced as Mae looked at Roger attentively. "What the hell," she finally said. "If your boy ain't old enough for a beer, he ain't old enough for anything else fun. And fun's what I think of when I look at him."

When she left Sheriff said, "Looks like you made a conquest."

Roger blushed. "Yeah, well, I'm pretty good at that, I guess." He smiled shyly at his father. "Must be in my genes."

The beers were brought and served. The men sipped at the frosted glasses. Michael put down his beer, took a deep breath, and said, "All right. I guess it's time you and I talked, Roger. Time for you to tell me what's been going on."

At that moment, a slight hardness came into Roger's gaze. It frightened his father. "Since you walked out, you mean?" Roger asked.

Michael didn't trust himself to answer aloud.

"There's not much," said Roger slowly, after a few moments. "Really not much. Just getting by. Going to school. Okay grades I guess, but I never had to try for that. Made the basketball team, but didn't keep it up. Coach was a bastard . . ." He looked up with a slightly apprehensive glance—the first time he'd cursed before his father. Sheriff made no movement, and Roger went on: "Got into some trouble . . ."

"What kind of trouble?" Sheriff asked, trying to keep the anxiety out of his voice.

"Penny-ante stuff. Just . . . stuff. You know. Nothing on my record though," he added with a bitter irony. "Mommy was dating this cop. Mommy dated a lot."

That said a lot to Michael Sheriff. He realized, with something like a blow, what it must have been like for the boy all these years. All these years when he wasn't there.

"I made it through all that time by thinking of you," said Roger, simply. "I've been planning this trip to see you since the day I figured out that you weren't ever coming back. Now I'm here. Except now I don't know what to do."

"What do you want to do?"

There was a lingering silence. "I liked running this morning," Roger admitted. "That was great. I want to do other things with you. I . . . I don't like myself very much right now." Now he looked up at his father. His eyes were bright and clear. "I've done some pretty rotten stuff. I've just been reacting to things around me. Don't like your teachers? Fuck 'em. Get by with a C when you know you could get an A. Coach push you too hard? Drop the team. You and your

friends like dope? Start pushing yourself, and you got all the
friends and all the cash you want . . ."

Sheriff blanched. *Selling drugs?* Michael Sheriff had
killed pushers. Shot them dead in the alleyways where they
lived and conducted business and spread death. Sheriff was
afraid to reply, afraid of what he might say. He signaled
Mae for two more beers.

"I never gave up that idea of coming to see you," Roger
went on. "But it got to be like a dream. More and more like
a dream. Like guys are always talking about going to Alaska
and making money on the pipeline—that kind of dream.
Then some shit came down in Nevada. Heavy shit. I got
scared."

"What shit came down?" said Sheriff in a voice that was
almost strangled.

"This guy I know got busted. For pushing dope, and hell,
he didn't do anything but grass. Ten years in the state pen.
This judge decided to make an example of him. He was
small time—he was small time even when you compared
him to *me*. *Ten years*. Then my best friend, he got this girl
pregnant. He married her. So he's eighteen and he's got a
wife, and the kid's mentally retarded, and there's another
kid on the way. He works in a gas station seven-to-four, and
at night he's at Burger King, and on the weekends he's at a
carwash. Just to make ends meet. That could have been me.
I screwed that girl one time. That could have been me."

Michael Sheriff's mind was reeling. His son pushing
dope? His son in jail? His son saddled with a teenaged wife
and a brain-damaged child? His anger surfaced and was momentarily directed at Roger. He felt like standing up and
smacking the kid across the face. What an idiot to come so
close to ruining his life! But then another realization came
over Michael. Roger had spent the last ten years of his life
without a father's guidance. And that was nobody's fault but
Michael's own.

His mind went over all the elements. A mother with a re-
volving door on her bedroom, teachers interested only in
collecting their paychecks, growing up in Nevada sur-

rounded by tinsel and gambling, prostitution and drugs, nothing there to lean against, to test yourself against, nothing there to show you how and where to stand.

"I'm sorry," said Michael Sheriff. It was all he could think to say, and he knew it was wrong.

"I don't want you to be sorry!" Roger slammed a fist on the Formica tabletop. Beer sloshed out of their glasses. "I didn't come all the way from Nevada for an apology. I came here for something more. I—" Roger's words suddenly stopped. Michael Sheriff looked into his son's eyes. He saw tears brimming there. If Roger said another word, they'd overflow. Spill down his face. Splash on the tabletop.

It was a mercy that the food was delivered then. Mae, seeing that something was going on, was unnaturally silent. She put down the platters, and went quickly away, leaving the two men alone.

When he felt Roger had recovered, Michael Sheriff asked his son. "What do you want? Who do you want to be?"

"My father's son." The words were deceptively smooth. They came in soft tones. They carried the burden of honesty.

"I can't make you into some ideal of a son—some dream that exists only in my mind," Sheriff protested. Knowing all the time that was exactly what he wanted. What he had dreamed about.

"I *want* you to," said Roger. "It's what I *need*. I need someone to tell me what to do with my life. To tell me when what I'm doing is right. When it's wrong. Someone to slap me on the back when I do something right, and somebody to wallop me when I do something wrong."

Roger had just put into words Michael's own dream of fatherhood. Michael didn't dare touch it. He asked bluntly, "What do you know about me?"

Roger hesitated only a moment. "Just what she told me. You went to Vietnam. You weren't the same when you came back."

"Nobody was the same," Sheriff said. "Not after Vietnam."

"Then you did work for the government. She said it was top-secret crap. She always talked about that in a funny way. Like you were lying to her all the time. Like you really had a desk job and were just screwing your secretary."

"I was with the CIA," said Sheriff, hoping his son wouldn't push. He didn't want to remember the years lost in the bureaucracy and bullshit of the federal government. Nor did he want to dredge up the memories of the foolish things he'd done for those idiots in Washington—all in the name of democracy. As though those assholes knew what the word meant.

"I didn't think you lied," said Roger. "But then she said you quit that job too. That was right after you left us. She said you got some big-time job because there was always money. She was mad about that, because she couldn't complain."

Just like her, thought Sheriff.

"That's what I know," said Roger. "I used to save your Christmas cards but one day she found 'em and threw 'em away."

Sheriff shook his head. "You don't know much . . ."

"I know enough. I know I want to stay here with you."

It's not possible, Sheriff thought. He didn't dare say it aloud. This was his first meal in a restaurant in the company of his son. How could he spoil it? Every day they spent together would bring a hundred firsts. When the time came to send Roger away, how would he do it?

Roger saw that his father didn't respond to his stated desire to remain with him in Massachusetts. Hurt swept into his eyes, but he was brave. He turned the subject, affecting not to notice his father's lack of commitment. That bravery hurt Michael Sheriff more than any recriminations could have.

"You're not in the CIA now, though, right?"

"I work for a company called Management Information Services." Sheriff smiled—the name seemed so bureaucratic, so innocent.

"Is that like computers or something? Computers pay."

"There are lots of computers at MIS," said Sheriff, "but I don't have much to do with them. I'm sort of—" *sort of an assassin, sort of a hired killer, specializing in jungle warfare, and arctic warfare, and urban guerrilla warfare . . .* "—sort of a field rep for the outfit."

"You can't tell me, right?" said Roger.

Michael Sheriff shook his head.

"And you don't want me to ask?"

"That'd be better . . ."

"Then I won't," said Roger, proudly displaying his obedience to his father's wish. Then he looked up at his father over his glass of beer and grinned. "But goddamn, that job must *pay . . .*"

. . . 13

"A MAN NEEDS a basic wardrobe," Sheriff instructed his son. "If the clothes are good to begin with and they're taken care of, they'll last for years. And every year they'll look better."

Michael Sheriff's choice for a basic wardrobe may have been simple, but it wasn't cheap. He insisted on quality. Roger had never been in the kind of men's clothing store that his father took him to. They were given two salesmen all their own, with a tailor sitting in a corner of the dressing room—a tape around his neck and a slice of chalk in his fingers. Sheriff gave a short list to the senior salesman and simply said, "Do it right for the boy." So Roger got a dark conservative suit, a light-colored three-piece suit, a tweed sports jacket, and a blue blazer. Three pairs of woolen trousers, three belts, more than a dozen shirts, a half dozen ties, a minimum of plain gold jewelry, three pairs of dress shoes, and a cashmere overcoat.

"We'll have everything to you in a week, Mr. Sheriff," said the clerk.

Sheriff replied, "Thank you," and they walked out of the store.

"You didn't pay," Roger said incredulously. From glancing at the price tags, and making estimates, he knew that the purchases had come to nearly two thousand dollars.

"They know where to send the bill," said his father. "That was the first stop."

The second store was the other side of the moon from the

first. Andy's Surplus Store was a rough-and-tumble place. But Michael Sheriff was known there as well. "Hey Sheriff, you gonna shoplift my profits again?" Andropolous Propokious was a heavyset man who lorded over his tiny fiefdom in Cambridge with an eagle eye.

"Up yours, Greek. Gotta get my boy some gear."

"Your boy?" Andy's expression changed. "You shitting me?"

"My son, Roger." Michael Sheriff clapped an arm around Roger's shoulders.

"Hey, hey! We got serious business here." Andy pushed his big body down the crowded aisle. "It is your kid. Jesus Christ! I can see it." Andy studied Roger's face. "So what does he need I don't got?"

That was the start of a frantic hour unlike anything Roger had ever experienced. "He needs *everything?*" Andy exclaimed. "He'll *get* everything."

Andy screamed the whole time, and his father's voice matched the fat man's in volume. Roger finally understood that Andy couldn't talk in any lower voice, nor hear if the other person's voice were less than a yell.

"You want him to wear junk? You gotta be kidding. No cheap shit. Give 'im Hanes, at least Hanes. None of that faggy designer shit, though. Don't carry it anyway. Hanes or BVD."

"Only two dozen pair of briefs? Hell, boy's gonna bust through two dozen pairs of briefs in no time. Three, at least three."

"What you mean, you want that alligator crap? It's past. Definitely past. Just pocket tees, I tell you, that's what's next. Plain pocket tees."

But all the decisions, even if reached at ear-splitting decibel levels, were friendly. Michael Sheriff would say half-a-dozen button-fly Levi's, and Andy would grin and take off for the stockroom. Or he'd insist on four pairs of boots—one hiking, one construction, one black leather, and one dress—and the grin grew wider.

"Who is this guy?" Roger finally asked in bewilderment.

"An old friend," said Sheriff.

Then Roger realized something, though he didn't know by what process of reasoning he had come to such a conclusion. Andropolous Propokious was not simply a storeowner, any more than his father was simply a "traveling rep" for a company called Management Information Services. His father was still an agent, of one sort or another. And so was Andy, this fat man lugging boxes down from the stock loft at the back of the shop.

Roger surveyed the store. Fantasies of secret arms shipments floated through his mind. He imagined there was a stockpile right in the basement. Maybe there was a secret group of Greek freedom-fighters that was headquartered here, aided and abetted in their struggle by his own father. Then he shook his head—television movie stuff. The Greeks weren't fighting against anybody anymore.

But he couldn't look at the store the same way now. His gaze rested for a few moments on each of the clerks and other customers in Andy's and he reenvisioned them in new roles. That fat black woman was a member of a terrorist squad come to off them. Roger imagined himself throwing his body in the path of her bullets, heroically saving his father and his Greek ally from instant death.

Hey, my father's a secret agent!

A young guy over in the corner was really . . .

Roger froze. The dream disappeared. Cold metal seemed to pour into his veins. The teenaged guy over in the corner of the store was carrying a knife. Roger knew it. He had used the same kind of blade himself and had stored it in his boot in precisely that way.

Not playacting now, Roger looked around the store more attentively. The guy across from him dressed as a punk didn't look right. Roger studied him. The clothing, the image was off. The hair wasn't really cut, only combed to look punk. The ears weren't pierced, he wore clasped earrings. The clothes were too new. There was a bulge in the guy's chest.

A gun.

Roger looked around and saw his father disappear down a stairway, directly behind Andy, both of them arguing loudly over the merits of certain types of trousers and overalls. The two men Roger had already identified as dangerous were now exchanging looks with a third and then . . . with the fat black woman he had facetiously imagined as the enemy.

Four of them. Two clerks. Roger and one other customer, blithely and blindly pawing through a stack of folded army shirts. Was this to be a simple robbery? He didn't think so. Fat black women don't make good armed robbers. Armed robbers don't take the trouble to disguise themselves as punks. It was more than a simple robbery, he knew that. But what was he to do? How could he sound an alarm?

He didn't have to.

"Freeze!" Michael Sheriff shouted from the stock loft at the back of their heads. Somehow he had only faked going into the basement. In his hands was a snub-nosed automatic rifle. Even to Roger's uneducated mind, the thing looked very dangerous.

Andy appeared in the open doorway to the basement. Roger stood hypnotized by the danger all around him. He watched carefully as the four people looked first at the rifle Michael Sheriff carried, then at the revolver in Andy's hand. But they moved, almost imperceptively. They were sidling slowly toward one another and at the same time toward Roger.

RAT-A-TAT-TAT! Sheriff's automatic rifle spat out an ear-shattering series of bursts. Little explosions erupted all around the tables. To Roger's horror, the black woman let out a shriek, her ample breast gushing out blood where the bullets cut a line of death.

Roger was mesmerized. He had never seen death. Not up close. You smelled it. You smelled blood, and you smelled the shit that the dying person let go in fear. That's what was really different from the television movies. You smelled death, and you tasted it in your mouth, and it made you want to vomit.

The other three, all men, threw their arms into the air.

Their female compatriot lay weltering on the wooden floor of Andy's Surplus, and they knew the man holding the machine gun wouldn't hesitate to do the same to them. Roger assumed that they'd be herded together, and the police called. Court dates, and investigations—and what would happen to his father? Shooting down a woman in a retail establishment, what if—

The pistol in Andy's hand shot out three quick angry bullets. One after another the three men slumped to the floor. Two got it in the forehead, the third in the eye. Roger was horrified. The men had been standing with their arms upraised, effectively weaponless.

The two clerks moved quickly now. They opened a trapdoor in the floor with expert and obviously practiced motion. Ignoring Roger, they dragged the four corpses to the new opening and shoved them down. Each body sent up a dull *thump* as it hit the basement floor. In less than a minute from his father's *"Freeze!"* the two clerks were spilling sawdust over the blood on the floor, and they and Andy had lighted cigars—to cover the noisome stench of powder and blood and shit and death. The customer who had been pawing through a stack of army shirts was long gone.

In another minute, two policeman came warily into the store. They looked around hesitantly. "Listen," one of the cops said to the clerk at the register, "we just got this weird report—"

But he was cut off by Andy yelling, at the top of his lungs, "What kind of man buys Fruit of the Loom for an eighteen-year-old son? How you expect that kid to hold up his head in a locker room, hunh?"

Roger looked out of the car window. After what he'd just witnessed, the placid scenery of the Boston suburbs seemed menacing somehow. Terrorists behind every screened door. Bombs planted beneath cars in driveways. Crossing guards palming hand grenades.

"Want to talk about it?" Michael Sheriff finally spoke. A certain fear gripped him. He was frightened of being judged by his son. For ten years he had lived and breathed only for the satisfaction of a job well done, that and the possibility of a nod of gratitude and approval from the Chairman. But he hadn't been judged. Certainly not by anyone whose opinion mattered to him.

Roger heard the words. He tried to form a response. He didn't want to say the wrong thing, but what was the right thing? "You're my father," he said at last.

"And you just saw your father shoot a woman down with a machine gun. Not pleasant," he said grimly.

"No," agreed Roger. "Not pleasant. She would have killed you, right?"

"That's what she was there for," Sheriff admitted. "She would have killed you, too, of course. That woman never did leave a witness. Ever. She once stabbed a blind man."

"Why were the other three killed? They could have been arrested, they could—"

"They were murderers," Sheriff said simply. "And they had diplomatic immunity. So they *couldn't* have been arrested." He decided to be truthful. "It was my job to get them," said Sheriff.

"You were expecting them?"

Sheriff looked at his son. "You think I would have exposed you to that kind of danger? You think I *wanted* you to see something like that? That's why Andy fired those three shots at the end. Because he didn't want a young man like you having to watch his father shoot down four people in cold blood. That's why. But if Andy hadn't done it, Roger, I would have. Because that was my job, and I couldn't have let anything interfere with that. Not even the fact that you were there watching."

They were silent for a few minutes. Then Roger asked curiously, "Don't you ever get caught?"

The question seemed so bizarre to Michael Sheriff that he laughed aloud. "In my business," he replied, "you don't get punished for killing somebody. You get punished for *not* killing somebody. You get the death penalty for that. Because they kill you instead. Do you understand?"

Roger nodded after a moment. "Your whole life is like that, isn't it?"

"Yes," said Sheriff. "My whole life."

"Then I guess I better get used to it," Roger said quietly.

14

THE KINDU LEADER grinned broadly at the sight in front of
him. Next to him stood the leader of the Europeans. The
Czech, whose name was Lukas Paloucky, looked on with
what might have been either indifference or stoicism. Stoicism if it mattered to him what misery he had caused, indifference if he didn't care. Neither man appeared moved by
the riotous noise of grief that surrounded them.

They stood on the edge of the Fashanti village. That way
they were out of reach of the flames that engulfed every hut.
Women were attempting to drag the aged and the infirm
from the rapidly burning structures, their wailing infants im-
peding their efforts by tugging at their mothers' skirts. Older
children huddled in the bushes surrounding the clearing.

The ten Fashanti men of that tiny, unnamed village were
chained together by their necks. It was the first taste of misery in their lives as slaves to the Kindu.

The only mercy of those lives in abject servitude would be
their brevity. Kindu slaves were short-lived.

Before these Fashanti men went, however, they had to
witness not just the physical devastation of their hamlet, but
also suffer the humiliation of Kindu mastery. They trembled
silently as their boy children were brought before them.

One man, once a hunter, now naked and chained, tried to
bolt from the group when his own young son was presented
by the Kindu raiders. The boy was no more than seven years
old. As the chains restrained him and made his opposition
futile, the hunter's ears were assailed by his son's fearful

cries and pleas for rescue. The hunter was forced to witness
the gleam in the eye of the Kindu warrior who held the
youngster by his wrists.

The boy's cries suddenly intensified as the Kindu lifted
him up in the air. Startled terror took over. Then the Kindu
lifted back his sword and in one swift terrible motion raced
it forward, severing the boy's body at the waist. Blood
poured out of both halves, blood and organs. His tiny quiv-
ering legs fell to the ground, but his upper torso and head—
still bearing a look of intelligent surprise—was poised for a
moment on the edge of the Kindu sword. His lungs and
stomach, pink and purple, sagged out on either side of the
sword blade. Then death came, merciful, and glazed over
the boy's eyes.

The upper half of the child toppled backward and fell directly before his father. Even then, as a final indignity, the
child's skull split open on a rock, and his brain gushed out
over his father's naked feet.

The Fashanti men were stunned by this brutality. All their
desire to fight ebbed away. Now, knowing their defeat, they
wanted only for all this to be over. For the village to be
burned to the ground. For themselves to be led away. Before
any more atrocities were forced on their unwilling vision.

Ashamed of their capture and their impotence, they refused to look across the village clearing to the other group of
captives. But to furtive glances the women appeared as if in
a dream: rising heat from the burning huts made their
women seem to shimmer in the bright noon light.

Boy children were useless to the Kindu. They had no intention of keeping them around. It took food to keep a boy
alive, and boys had the troublesome habit of nurturing rebellion in their hearts. Boy children would take up a spear
against their oppressors just as soon as they were able to lift
it. Boy children were—for the most part—worthless.

But the Kindu were perfectly happy to let young girls survive. All the females, of any age under twenty, had been
spared. Those over that age had been judged too old for con-
cubines and summarily dispatched, usually with a long knife

sawed once across the throat. In shocked astonishment at the slaughter of their brothers and mothers, the young girls stood now in a group. All had been stripped. The Kindu would occasionally walk over to them. From the beginning, the girls understood that protests or resistance would be useless. Now, cowering in fear, they let the alien hands probe them, lift and weigh their breasts, knead their buttocks, evaluate their sex.

The girls, some as young as ten years, were treated no differently than the older females. Never introduced to the mysteries of sex till now, they were as quickly and as often subjected to the taunts and violations of the Kindu as the rest. They didn't know—but they would soon find out—that the Kindu treasured the bodies of youngsters. The Kindu sometimes raided only to replenish their supply of nubile and tender female flesh.

A handful of small boys stood with the young women and girls. These eight-, nine-, and ten-year-old boys would be spared death, for all their faces were fresh, and their bodies were smooth and unmarked. But these unfortunate boy children would be sacrificed to the same perverted appetite as their sisters. And that was one more humiliation for the fathers on the other side of the clearing: to go into slavery knowing that the male offspring of their loins would be changed into she-males, for the indulgences of the Kindu.

Still, in the face of the carnage and destruction around them, the women drew back in a special kind of disgust and loathing when the two white-skinned men approached. The two Czechs, Otokar Hron and Jurek Theer, wore leering smiles. Hron's face was terribly scarred. He moved through the crowd and seemed intent on jamming a finger or two up into the sex of every huddling female. He enjoyed the sharp pain and humiliation he caused with his motions. He would linger if a girl's expression was especially reactive. If a once proud woman cried tears at the degradation she endured at his hand, Hron made sure she had to endure it all the longer.

His compatriot Theer had a way that was a little more discerning. The frightened women in the front of the group had no charm for him. He only became interested when he found the cluster of the youngest girls in the rear. One, a tiny thing much too young for breasts or pubic hair, was his reward for patience. When he found her, Theer let out a long whistle of pleased discovery.

Otokar Hron laughed, for he knew what that whistle meant.

The child shivered in dread at Theer's approach, but her fear only heightened his interest. His hand reached out and caressed her cheek. She pulled back in alarm. He slapped her hard on just the spot where he first had touched her so softly. Then Theer smiled. In his mind the slap was more pleasing than the fondling indulgence.

The color of her skin displeased him. Not that the racial identity made that much difference to him, really. It was just that her skin was so dark he'd be deprived of that special pleasure he got in watching bruises develop. Scandinavian girls were so much better at that—those and the Dutch. They marked so easily and with such varied color.

But the fear in this one was more than adequate for pleasure. Theer could just imagine how she would squirm, how much she would attempt to fight his approaches that night. How much she would be punished.

Theer turned and spoke to one of the Kindu warriors, using the multilingual driver as a translator. There was no problem in securing this girl for his use. The Kindu were delighted that his interest would now be diverted from their own female children to this slave. She would have a short life in any event.

The Kindu chief had moved over to see the action in the circle of women. He enjoyed the Fashanti women's response to the Czechs. So, they didn't like to be fondled by foreigners? It gave him an idea. He spoke sharply to one of his men who immediately gathered others and ran to fulfill the chief's command.

The open-air temple of the Fashanti village hadn't yet been touched by the flames. Arranged on stone pedestals with great care and honored respect, the small ebony and bronze-cast statues and fetishes of the Fashanti gods stood in silent watch over the ruination of the hamlet. The laughing Kindu tossed and knocked over most of the antique statues as they sought their goal. The Fashanti men turned away from this final desecration of the meaning of their lives. They didn't see that the Kindu had found what they were looking for.

The Kindu each grabbed a couple of the statues and ran with them to the chief; he was handed one to inspect. It was a three-foot carved fetish, representing Lakati, the Fashanti god of fertility. The statue was made of brass, and marked with an incredibly large phallus, the carved penis as long as the statue was tall. Lakati, in fact, was leaning far backward with both arms wrapped around his phallic member, and it was only in this manner that the fetish was balanced enough to stand upright. The chief turned and went to the first woman.

One of the Kindu warriors grabbed the woman's waist and held her motionless. The chief howled with laughter at her horror as she began to understand what he was going to do. Lakati's erect member was painfully rammed up into her dry and unwilling sex. She shrieked, only to have the chief begin to manipulate the statue inside her.

The young wife, feeling herself defiled beyond measure, tried to beat back the chief. He might have killed her on the spot for such rebellion, but an idea came to him. He took the fetish and held it for several minutes over the still-burning fire of the one of the hut foundations. The brass statue took on heat. Then the Kindu chief repeated the operation with the statue of Lakati—but this time it was fatal. She screamed and screamed, until at last she died.

This was the wife of the man who had seen his son cut in half on the edge of the Kindu sword. The boy had been her firstborn son.

The Fashanti hunter had watched his son and his wife die deaths as cruel as any he had ever heard of, in a long life spent in the jungles of Leikawa. With a sudden and complete commitment to the act, he knew he must die.

The metal collar around his neck was joined to those of the men directly in front of and behind him. He gauged their strength and he sensed the power of the collar. With a quick motion he jumped, purposely leaving his neck as vulnerable as possible. In the air, he drew his legs up to his chest and clasped his arms about them. As he fell, he hoped that the chain would pull taut, and his neck would snap within the metal collar.

But that didn't happen. The man in front of him, seeing what was happening, dropped to the earth, and the crazed, mourning hunter simply crumpled unhurt on the ground. There he lay and wept for his wife and his son, and there he remained as the Kindu came and laughed.

15

MICHAEL SHERIFF'S HAPPINESS continued for six more days.

Time was the only constraint on what father and son shared with one another. Sheriff found himself bounding out of bed and rousing Roger at the break of dawn. Or at least going into find Roger already dressed and waiting for him, sleepy-eyed, staring out the window at the rising sun behind pink and yellow clouds.

They ran every morning. In the late afternoon they went through the grueling physical exercises that were Michael's daily routine. Even when Sheriff told him it wasn't necessary, Roger pushed himself to extremes in order to match his father's every move. When his muscles screamed in pain the following morning, Roger denied the agony. If his father caught the expression of sharp discomfort on his face, Roger answered, "No pain, no gain," and went on.

Desperate to discover the inner workings of one another's minds, they seemed to consume one another. Sheriff insisted on taking Roger to a record store. "What music do you like?" he demanded.

"What do *you* like?" Roger insisted in return. This scenario was replayed in bookstores, supermarkets, restaurants, until they finally realized that only one thing sufficed for happiness—the presence of the other.

Each learned to identify the smell of the other's sweat during their workouts. They memorized the harsh breathing of their lungs during runs. Michael studied the way that

Roger ate, the manner of his chewing, what he ate first and what he ate last, how he held knife and fork. Roger saw— and when he was alone, practiced—Michael's secure stride.

Everything they did for those days was an echo of the chorus each was singing in his mind.

This is my father.

This is my son.

Now the time was drawing to an end. Roger was insistent that he would handle it as a man. He took the last day and made it into a period of study for the future. He had been following Michael's lead in the workouts. Now he sat his father down and insisted on recording the exact number of reps for each exercise. What did Michael think he should read while he was gone? What did Michael think he should do about . . .

"Stop it! I'm not going to be in Africa forever!" The constant preparations on that last day drove Sheriff mad with a frustration he had never before experienced. For he knew there was an adjunct to that promise. He wouldn't be in Africa forever, true enough. *But he might come back in a mahogany box.*

At least one of the reasons for his effectiveness in the field had been his total fearlessness. Now, with someone to come home to, would he start to take precautions that would, in the end, doom him? Could he maintain his peak awareness with this unusual distraction always rising up in his mind? When an enemy raised his rifle, what would Sheriff be thinking about? About the preservation of his life? Or about Roger's plans for college? When you thought about your wife, when you were afraid for your kid, when you imagined that someone was going to get through to your girl— that's when your step faltered. That's when you failed to trust your instinct. That's when you didn't take that one step out into the open that would give you a clear shot at the man who wanted to blow you out of your shoes.

Back in Massachusetts, doing his sit-ups, would Roger be the innocent cause of his father's death?

In the morning—the last morning—Roger drove his father

to Logan Airport. The Volvo was parked, the orders given, the bomb activated.

Roger had to stay within the compound for the entire time Michael was gone. The groundsman or Katrina would get him anything he needed. But he mustn't leave under any circumstances. Michael hadn't had time to teach Roger the response to danger. Or, even more important, to teach the boy how to sense when danger was near.

Roger didn't argue. He had been at Andy's Surplus. He knew his father wasn't talking about boogeymen or third-rate hoods who got drunk once a year and broke somebody's leg. There were people out there with guns and knives and God knew what other kind of shit. They didn't have consciences and they weren't scared of getting caught.

Roger vowed that when his father took the next trip, Michael Sheriff wouldn't have to worry about his son's safety. By that time, Roger would know how to take care of himself. It had come as a little shock to him that his father wouldn't even allow him to drive the Volvo the fifteen miles home from the airport.

Inside the terminal, just before the security inspection, Michael Sheriff and his son stood aside. They looked at one another for a moment, then Roger said, in a broken voice, "I've waited a long time for you. Please come back."

Sheriff wrapped his arm around Roger's shoulder and pulled hard, almost as if he were going to squeeze Roger's entire body against his heart. He said nothing.

After Sheriff went through the security gate, passing through the briefcase that contained maps and documents on Leikawa, he turned and held up a hand to his son.

Roger was grinning. "You forgot to tell me—how do I get home?"

Sheriff laughed. He was reaching into his pocket for a couple of twenties to hand over to Roger when his smile froze on his face. He withdrew his hand, and then simply pointed down the corridor behind Roger.

Roger turned. The Chairman stood a few feet behind him wearing a rather sporty tweed suit.

"Good trip," he said briefly to Michael Sheriff. "I'll see that the boy gets home safely."

16

MICHAEL SHERIFF WATCHED the stewardess coming down the aisle of the first-class section, flashing her toothpaste smile as she handed out the violet and black sleep blinders. When she came to his seat the expression on her face changed only the slightest bit. But it changed in a way that Sheriff identified very quickly.

This one's going to be easy, he thought to himself. The presence of a woman in heat seemed appropriate. It would make the transition back to working easier. Besides, he'd spent the past ten days almost exclusively in Roger's company. After that long, Michael Sheriff knew that his body was aching for the kind of release you didn't get with a five-mile morning run, or a hundred sit-ups in the afternoon, or a whiskey and soda after dinner.

"Blinders?" the stewardess asked with a smile that, for once, seemed genuine.

"No," Sheriff replied, "I'll be up the whole trip."

For the next half hour he toyed with her. The wide seat gave him an opportunity to spread his legs so that she could have a good view of the mound between his thighs. When he saw her coming closer he allowed his hand to drape down to his crotch. The very act of enticing her was exciting him. He knew that the sight of what he had waiting for her would have turned her attention to that part of his body anyway, but the lingering hand made sure she glanced in that direction.

And she did. Every chance she had.

When she brought him his first drink he stretched, letting his arms splay out into the air. Then he scratched his chest through his shirt, separating the cloth to reveal the thick hair beneath.

It was almost cruel the way that he played with her. For the next hour she passed his seat every few minutes. Drinks and snacks came to him continuously and gratis while her other passengers waited for even the most minor service. He knew it was time to act when he looked up and watched her run her tongue over her lower lip.

There were few women that Michael ever had to work to get. This wasn't one of them. But she was nice, he had to admit that. She had long brown hair gathered up on top of her head. Her little stewardess cap, which would have been very silly anywhere in the world but in the interior of a jetliner, was perched there precariously. Her uniform skirt was tight; the hips underneath it were just wide enough to interest him. The buttocks were full and invited his serious attention.

The plane was over the Atlantic. It was night but the moon had not yet risen over the disc of the earth. Most of the passengers had already put on their sleep masks and were at least trying to get the jump on jet lag.

It was time to make his move.

He stood and headed toward the restroom. He had timed it perfectly. No one saw when he nodded to her, firmly and only once. He knew she'd be waiting for the signal, and he didn't have to make it any clearer than that.

Leaving the door to the toilet cracked open, he stood against the wall with his arms crossed over his chest. He didn't have long to wait. He checked his watch. In less than a minute she entered, closing and locking the door behind her.

She fell into his arms, reached up to grab his shoulders. He wasted no time. This wouldn't be one of the long luxurious encounters. Not on a plane flying several miles above the Atlantic Ocean. He let her nuzzle his chest just long enough to get that part of the business out of her system.

Then he lifted her up and sat her on the washbasin stand. His hands went to her breasts and felt the softness through her jacket and blouse. "You're awfully rough," she said, but there was no complaint in her voice. His hands moved down and up under her skirt. He could feel the heat coming from between her legs. He made a mental bet with himself that she was already wet and ready for him.

He pulled at her panties, but the quarters were so cramped that there was no way for him to ease them off. With both hands he grabbed the fabric, and tugged until it ripped.

The stewardess drew in her breath with a hiss between her teeth.

Each half of her torn panties fell down and caught on one of her ankles.

He pulled back for a moment and unzipped his pants. He was already hard with anticipation. He was used to women being appreciative when they saw what he was going to give them and the little stewardess didn't disappoint him. When the whole length of his erection was released from its bondage she reached down and touched it. Her tiny, soft palm ran up and down the shaft and then almost reverently lingered on the thick, angrily red head.

She started to speak, then thought better of it, and closed her mouth with a satisfied smile.

He placed his hands under her buttocks and dragged her to the edge of the stand. She opened herself willingly.

He let her guide him inside her. He won the bet with himself. She was soaking with excitement. He pushed her hand away, and glided in with one long, slow, single motion until he could feel their pubic hair mesh. He was rewarded with a deep, probably unconscious, sigh from her.

Sheriff liked to have sex with firm motions. He liked using his manhood to bring out the most passionate response a woman could give. He knew that this meant he had to let her measure him by inches. He glided himself in and out of the hot fleshy portal of her body, making certain she always knew exactly how far he had traveled.

Soon he had her clutching at his chest. Her fists flailed

and knocked against the sides of the tiny, claustrophobic compartment. Then they gathered up his hair and tugged, as though she were trying to give back to him the intensity of the sensation she was receiving. He ignored the way she tore at his hair. Instead he plied her body with his tool with as much skill and instinct as if they had made love a thousand times before. She started to pant with the obvious beginning of her orgasm; when it hit her she buried her mouth against his bare chest. He could feel, though not hear, her scream.

Michael Sheriff took pride in sex. It was a point of honor with him that every woman he was with remembered him, and remembered him well. He never let his own pleasure escape from his self-control. And he wasn't the man to go half-measures in anything he did.

He let her orgasm clutch his manhood with its spasms. Then, without giving her any rest, he started up again. He looked down and watched as his flesh invaded her, then retreated only to return once again into the moist sheath.

"Oh no," she whispered in alarm. Her feeble protest was partly a surrender to what she knew was going to happen to her. It was also a cry of alarm, knowing the second orgasm would be even more powerful than the first. She pressed the palms of her hands against the sides of the cubicle and rocked from side to side with the rhythm of Sheriff's thrusts, almost as if she were trying to break them out of the confined space. Their hot commingled breath filled the room, and began to steam the mirrors.

Only when he felt her coming again did Michael let his pace pick up enough to ensure that he would join her orgasm. He felt himself move faster and then still faster. Now, as he shoved the whole length of himself up her, her cries of protest took on some authenticity. Women were always complaining about his size. They always made some protest about taking it all inside them. Those protests Sheriff never believed—but cries such as this stewardess was making were something else. Those he believed in.

When he began to feel as if his entire pelvic region were boiling, Sheriff sent a final few thrusts at her. He watched her mouth open in an honest mixture of pain and pleasure. When her second orgasm gripped him, his own took over and sent pulsing waves of his masculinity pumping inside her.

She thrust her frail wrist into her mouth to stifle her scream.

A few moments later, while Sheriff buttoned his shirt and smoothed his hair, the stewardess tried to regain herself. Her breathing was still irregular, her eyes glazed, her uniform in complete disarray.

Michael finally put away his receding manhood and zipped up his pants. He settled back into his seat with another gratis Scotch.

17

THEY ALWAYS looked the same.

It could have been London or Tokyo, San Francisco or Rabat. It didn't make any difference. Michael Sheriff spotted him here in Zuubata just as easily as he would have in the other places.

It was at least partially the bland look of his face. There was no character in it. The man looked like a candidate for a training program at a bank or insurance company. The clothing was just as lacking in distinction, except that here in Zuubata it looked too good. The creases were too well kept for a tropical city, the shirt too crisp. Probably changes five times a day just to make sure the sweat doesn't show through, Sheriff thought.

There was some little hope that the clean-shaven blond man wasn't waiting for him. Clinging to that slim unlikelihood, Sheriff walked straight past him, heading toward the customs lines at the other side of the terminal room.

But the guy was looking for Michael Sheriff and no one else. That asshole Flank probably tipped them off. Flank was just the kind of jerk who got his rocks off spilling information to the CIA.

"Sheriff, I want to talk to you." The delivery of the words betrayed a military background. Sheriff stopped and stared at the man. He reached inside his shirt pocket and pulled out one of his Sobranies. *Probably should stop smoking. Bad example for the kid.* Sheriff lighted the black tobacco, still not speaking to the CIA operative.

Only when he exhaled the smoke did the CIA man appear to realize that Sheriff's indifference to him wasn't feigned. "We'd like to invite you to the embassy. For a little chat."

"No thank you," said Sheriff, and turned to walk away.

"Come on, Sheriff," said the man, jerking along a step or two, and then grabbing Sheriff by the arm.

Michael stopped, turned, and stared at the man's hand. The operative let go, looking a little foolish. However, he didn't apologize. "Come on, Sheriff, don't give me a hard time. You know we have ways."

"Do you?" said Sheriff. "Then try them."

The operative hesitated.

"Nothing up your sleeve right now?" asked Sheriff. "Then I guess I have to wait to see what you come up with."

"The ambassador wants to talk to you."

"Tell the ambassador to send me an engraved invitation and I'll consider it," said Sheriff. "And to make things easy, I'll tell you where I'm staying. The Sheraton."

The air conditioner worked at the Zuubata Sheraton. So, evidently, did everything else. The ability of American corporations to recreate themselves in every clime, and under the auspices of any political regime, was one of the wonders of the modern world. A Sheraton in Zuubata had the same soap as the hotel in Bangkok; the same sheets as the hotel in Oslo; the same carpets as the hotel in Detroit. And probably the same bland food as all the rest of them.

There was a knock at the door. Sheriff left his perch near the big picture window that looked out over the sprawling slums of the city and went to answer the summons. He opened the door and found a smiling black bellboy. His errand was obvious from the small tray he held in a soiled white glove.

The bellboy's white gloves were soiled in the West Kensington Sheraton, too, Sheriff remembered.

Sheriff dug in his pocket and found some coins. He tipped the very pleased employee and took the linen envelope off

the tray. Sheriff took the stationery over to the chair by the
window. He tore open the flap, and inside found a folded
piece of thick vellum, formally inscribed:

HER EXCELLENCY
MRS MARGARET DURRELL
AMBASSADOR
OF THE UNITED STATES OF AMERICA
TO THE REPUBLIC OF LEIKAWA
REQUESTS THE PRESENCE OF
MICHAEL SHERIFF, ESQ
FOR DINNER
AT THE AMERICAN EMBASSY
THIS EVENING
EIGHT O'CLOCK P.M.

Her Excellency! Well, even though it wasn't engraved, the
embassy seal was embossed on red wax.

But wasn't there a bit of an insult in leaving off the RSVP,
or not providing a messenger in case of a decline? They
were assuming he'd be there.

Sheriff decided to go. Maybe the embassy had a decent
chef.

Mrs. Margaret Durrell was waiting in the formal living
room of the embassy when Sheriff showed up at the ap-
pointed hour. The building had once been the home of one
of Leikawa's colonial masters—a man who had made his
fortune in the exploitation of the rare woods of Leikawa's
jungles. He had exploited not a few natives along the way.
The rain forest of southern Leikawa wasn't the healthiest
place in the world, especially if your employer decided that
his Swiss bank account couldn't afford the luxury of medical
supplies for his workers. When Leikawa gained its independence, the lumber magnate decamped to Central America,
where there were more rain forests and enough impover-
ished Indians to work them. But before he left Leikawa, this
millionaire made one last killing.

He sold his home to the Unites States government for twice its worth. The cost accountants balked at first, but the millionaire quite justly pointed out that it would cost three times as much to build a similar structure, once bribes to Zuubata and Leikawa officials were figured in. The millionaire later regretted his generosity. The Russians bought a mansion down the street, and paid five times its value.

"Mr. Sheriff."

The woman who stood and extended a hand toward Michael Sheriff was about his own thirty-eight years of age. Her hair was impeccably coiffed; he imagined she'd brought her own hairdresser to Leikawa. This was no native job. Margaret Durrell's skin was taut, evidence of a lot of athletic activity. Probably tennis. Her figure was trim and well-shaped, her dress plain, and plainly expensive. Two trips a year to Neiman-Marcus or Bergdorf Goodman, Sheriff surmised, and probably dropped ten thousand at a time.

Those were guesses. In his mind, he went over the facts he'd learned about her when he typed out a query on the portable computer he always carried with him to access MIS data banks.

Margaret Durrell. Dallas, Texas. Daughter of Theodore Durrell, founder and now Chairman of the Board of Durrell Petroleum. Born, Dec. 1, 1945. Happy childhood. B.A. Tulane University, 1963. University of Virginia Law School, 1966. Private practice and constant attendance at Dallas charity events until two years ago when, in reward for substantial political contributions to presidential incumbent, was given post of first American ambassador to the Republic of Leikawa. Long-term, emotional involvement with private secretary, Vera Kormivan, born of Russian immigrant parents. CIA connection for both women nearly certain.

The MIS report didn't do her justice, because it didn't mention her eyes. They were pale green and cold, and hostile toward both him and his mission in Leikawa.

She made no small talk. "Sheriff," she said bluntly, "I don't enjoy the idea of an unattached hotshot coming into my territory and upsetting things. Leikawa operates on a delicate balance. You've got two feet that weigh ten tons apiece.''

"What makes you think I'm unattached?" said Sheriff. "You must know—"

"MIS," Margaret Durrell interrupted with a sneer. "I know all about MIS and the Chairman, and I've seen grown men play games before. Let me tell you that, so far as I'm concerned, Michael Sheriff, the Chairman, and every disaffected Vietnam vet employed by Management Information Services is completely unattached from political, social, and economic reality.''

"Are you going to force me out of the country?"

"You'd sneak back in. Leikawa has two thousand miles of border with six different nations. They maintain a border patrol of six men, and one of them is deaf. No, I'm not going to turn you around on the next plane out. I'm going to make a deal with you."

Sheriff was silent. He sipped the excellent bourbon she'd poured out for him.

"A deal to share information."

"You get information," Sheriff said. "And I get what?"

"You get me off your back is what you get," said the ambassador to Leikawa, and poured herself a glass of bourbon as well. "And if you refuse to cooperate, I won't personally scotch-tape wasps to your nuts in the middle of the night— but I have friends who will. My friends have other tricks too. There's not a lot for an ambassador to occupy herself in this shit-hole of a country, so I sit behind my big desk upstairs and think up things to do to men I don't like. I tell you, Sheriff," said the ambassador, touching the palm of her hand lightly to her sprayed hair, "this heat does something to a woman's brain."

Sheriff still didn't reply.

The ambassador, as if assuming that his silence was acquiescence, went on: "I want to know exactly why you're here. Exactly what you intend to do. How you think you're going to get it done. I want to know where you go, and I want an X on the map every time you stop to take a shit. You got me? You got what I'm talking about, and what I need from you?''

"I got it," said Sheriff.

"Am I going to get it?" Margaret Durrell demanded.

"Can I give you my answer after dinner?" Sheriff asked.

"I get the answer now," she said.

"The answer is no," said Sheriff. "I stay unattached. I'm playing this game alone."

"Get out."

"I have an invitation to dinner."

"Withdrawn," said the American ambassador to Leikawa. "And you'd better start sleeping with one hand over your balls, Sheriff."

Michael Sheriff had to concede that, for a diplomat, Margaret Durrell talked pretty straight.

18

THE SOUND of mourning changes from culture to culture. Every people has its means of expressing grief. It might be the theatrical cries and wailings of the Jews at the ancient wall in Jerusalem, the misleading laughter of the Irish at a wake, the dignified keening of Japanese mothers—but the human ear can always identify the real sorrow and grief behind the ritualized display.

That sense of mourning was heavy over Fashata. In this, the largest village of the Fashanti, women crouched in a large circle in the village square and cried aloud while the men stood behind them, their faces frozen in masks that refused to acknowledge the sorrow they felt as sharply as the women.

Michael Sheriff stood on the outskirts of the gathering and watched. He had seen this kind of grief before. The Fashanti were mourning not only for a headman killed, but for the tribe itself. Sheriff began to understand how great a mission he had taken on for MIS and the Chairman.

He wondered at the way the people were gathered, in a circle, as though about an invisible leader. He moved closer, glad that his alien presence was ignored. Then he was able to see. Then he understood.

The eyes of the skull were opened in obscene sightlessness. The mouth gaped to greet swarms of buzzing flies. The man had obviously been murdered. Sheriff could see two bullet holes in the forehead that still bore tatters of black flesh.

He moved back, away from the circle. He returned to the jeep that had brought him to the interior of Leikawa. Prince Motala sat in the back seat of the vehicle, fanning away flies with an animal-hair whisk that was dyed yellow.

"These are your only hope?" Sheriff asked, spreading a hand back toward the gathering.

"Yes."

"I thought they were decent warriors. I saw no indication of that." The men who were mourning the murdered Fashanti headman had stood weaponless behind the line of wailing women.

"They were, Mr. Sheriff. They once ruled an enormous area of this country. They were the proudest of all the tribes. Now they have been domesticated, you might say. They've abandoned the old ways—and the protection the old ways afforded them. They've taken up the new ways but they don't know them well enough to use them entirely to their advantage. It's a difficult time in their transition. They can't yet protect themselves."

Sheriff looked back. The men stood straight. There was obvious strength in their bearing, in their straightforward gaze and motionlessness. Maybe there was something to work with. A hardness that could be turned into aggression against their enemies.

The prince spoke again. "This will go on for the day. We'll have to come back tomorrow. I will make the introductions then."

"No," Sheriff said. "I'll be coming back alone."

Sheriff returned to Fashata at dawn. He carried no weapon except a large hunting knife. That, and the knowledge the prince had given him over dinner in their tent the night before.

Fashata was a large village for the area, with a population of more than three thousand, the upper limit for communities as backward as those of Leikawa. A larger population tended to produce urban decay as pronounced as anything you might see in the South Bronx, though of course on a much smaller scale. Fashata was connected to the rest of

Leikawa only by footpaths and a single road so bad that the
prince's jeep had had trouble making the journey. There was
no railway, no airport, and the river within a few hundred
yards of the town was filled with unnavigable rapids. So despite the eagerness of the Fashanti for improvements,
Fashata looked very much as it had a hundred years before.

Except that you could buy Levi's blue jeans in the open-
air market.

The men of Fashata were only two steps deep into Western civilization. They felt the jungle breathing at their
backs.

And that was the best news Sheriff had heard since he arrived in Africa.

As he walked toward the village square where he had seen
the exposed skull of the Fashanti headman the day before,
Sheriff was conscious of the heads that peeked out of the
mud-brick buildings hodgepodged around.

It was the type of architecture that prevailed in the swath
of land that lay between the Sahara and the more southernly
jungles of Africa. Here the dry season had precedence, but
there was sufficient rain to sustain agriculture and hold together the mud bricks.

But for how long?

Sheriff knew what the Fashanti didn't—that the Sahara
was creeping southward, hectare by hectare, choking the
lungs of Africans and starving their bellies. The statistics of
deaths were unimaginable to Americans. Thirty-nine thousand infants dead in Ethiopia alone in a single year—dead
because the desert sand was now drifting over acreage that a
year before had been fertile fields and productive pasture.

Leikawa was going to need that export money from the
cobalt and the uranium. Without it, the country had maybe
another ten or twenty years before deaths started to outnumber births. Only those mineral resources finally stood between Leikawa and extinction. The Saharan sands would
make the fatalities of a hundred years of tribal warfare insig-
nificant by comparison. But how to explain so vast a change
to a people who had a concept of geography that was little

more advanced than Here/Not Here; Wet Season followed the Dry Season; Good Crop followed a Bad Crop, sometimes two Good Crops in a row? But it was nearly impossible to convince the Fashanti that soon Dry Season would follow Dry Season, and Bad Crop follow Bad Crop forever.

United Nations planners could chart the expansion of the Sahara, but the natives of Africa weren't going to be persuaded till the hot lifeless sand had covered them over. Sheriff wasn't contemptuous of the Africans. If an ice age ever came again, New Englanders would sit in their well-insulated houses and maintain that the winter was merely a bitter one right up until those houses were crushed by advancing glaciers.

Sheriff wasn't going to try to convince the Fashanti of the evanescence of their climate and their way of life. He was going to give them the will to preserve it. If he could secure the mines for Leikawa, he would provide the means to hold on.

Sheriff reached the square in the center of the village. A lone woman knelt before the headman's skull—it would be his wife, according to the tradition that Prince Motala had explained to him. The decapitated head was little more than a bare white skull now, for the mourning widow had gone into the jungle and collected a special kind of flesh-eating beetle. These ravenous insects had now nearly done their work—several still cavorted in the eye sockets—and when they had eaten all the flesh, the widow would bring the cleaned skull to the house of the succeeding headman.

It was not hard for Sheriff to identify the headman's home: it was the largest structure fronting the square, and on one long plain wall was painted the red and black geometric figure indicative of Fashanti chieftainship. He knew, too, that he did not enter a headman's home unbeckoned. He would have to wait for his invitation.

The African sun bore down on him. His wide-brimmed green linen hat fought off the sun's intensity so that he didn't keel over; but it did nothing to stop the flow of sweat that first soaked his hair and then, saturating that, began to flow down his face and neck. The stains beneath his arms grew and grew till they met in the front and back of his cotton shirt. His briefs grew soaked at the waistband and around his thighs, and eventually water began to drip down his legs and into his boots. He was soaked outwardly, and dried up on the inside.

He waited more than an hour. He gauged time by the sun, not his watch. It would have been impolite to do that. If the men inside the house—he knew they were men by their voices—had seen him look at his watch, they might never have invited him in. In his line of work, there were always periods of waiting such as this. Sometimes you waited in comfortable circumstances, and sometimes you waited in uncomfortable circumstances. Sometimes your life depended on your alertness, sometimes you could let your mind wander. His mind wandered now, to Roger. Wondering what his son was doing. Wondering—

It occurred to Sheriff suddenly that he had never before had anything similar to think about in these times of waiting. No such lodestone for his thoughts. No such consolation in these periods of monotonous discomfort. Now he had Roger. And as he waited in the African sun to be invited inside a mud-brick house that probably wasn't much cooler anyway, Sheriff planned out his son's day for him. Every minute of it. And seemed to live it with the boy. And then almost laughed aloud, thinking, I'll raise Roger to be just like me. So he can stand around Africa wetting his trousers with perspiration.

About then an old woman came out of the portal to the shack. Her black skin was creased with wrinkles. She had no teeth but her gums were in perpetual motion, chewing on some plant that had dyed the interior of her mouth bright red. She barely bowed to Sheriff, then stood aside, waving her hand toward the entry. Sheriff withheld the sigh of relief he felt. The sun wasn't going to do anything but get higher and hotter. He, at least, could escape it now.

He bent over and went through the door. Masada Saku, the headman of Fashata, was waiting for him. The leader wore only a ceremonial loincloth. His old, bony legs and chest were bare. A necklace of yellow beads hung around his neck. Like Prince Motala, he idly beat a yellow switch across his shoulders, like a lazy penitent. The gesture was mere ritual, for Sheriff didn't detect any flies inside. Masada Saku's eyes, intensely bright, studied Sheriff. He spoke to Michael finally in a clear and barely accented English. "It's been many years since a European knew enough to observe the ways of our people."

Sheriff silently nodded.

A younger man sat on each side of Masada Saku, a little lower than him on his pillow. Each also wore a breechcloth, though their exposed bodies exhibited the muscles of manhood in full flower. Sheriff knew they were Masada Saku's sons. They too studied Sheriff, with less formality than their father, though hardly with warmth.

For several moments, neither Sheriff nor Masada Saku spoke. The only sound was the rhythmic *whish* of the flyswatter on the old man's skin.

"Why have you come to the home of the headman of Fashata?" one of the sons asked, unable to contain his curiosity.

"To join the Fashanti in war." Sheriff spoke calmly, without bravado.

Nor was there any surprise in the response of Masada Saku. "We are a peaceful trible. We are citizens of Leikawa. We are not at war."

"Why then are widows gathering beetles for their dead husbands' skulls?"

The sons flinched. Masada Saku spoke: "That was the husband of my sister. He was headman of the neighboring village, as I am headman of Fashata. My sister's husband was the victim of human jackals and will be avenged. One hunts down jackals and kills them, one does not send them a declaration of war."

"Perhaps Fashanti warriors have forgotten what it is like to be at war," said Sheriff. "Perhaps it would be well for them to admit that."

All three male faces in front of him hardened. Three pairs

of eyes sent out a challenge to Sheriff that he was happy to
receive. The Fashanti were insulted. They were infuriated to
hear a European speak in this fashion.

But Masada Saku evidently also respected Michael Sheriff for his audacity. After a moment, he waved Sheriff toward a pillow that was covered in the customary blue fabric
woven by the Fashanti women. The headman signaled the
old woman who had been crouching in the shadows.

In a few moments she came forward with a tray of shallow pottery cups filled with steaming black coffee. Sheriff
took one of the cups and held it in both hands as he waited
for his hosts to be served. He lowered his head a few inches
in thanks to the headman, and then drank.

The coffee was like mud, an unstrained solution of
ground beans in barely tepid water. But it was what the
Fashanti drank, and what he'd drink too. He might have had
a harder time getting it down if Katrina hadn't been serving
it to him like that for the week preceding his departure.

"I know some things about you, Masada Saku," said
Sheriff after the formality of the coffee had been gone
through.

The old man appeared neither puzzled, curious, nor
frightened. "I know nothing of you," he said in return.
"You are a soldier, however."

"And I am here to fight with you," said Sheriff. "You
don't need to know any more about me than that."

Masada Saku took more coffee. His sons were clearly
holding back their own reactions to Sheriff. Their respect for
their father and tradition built Sheriff's hope for this enter-
prise. Masada Saku spoke again. "What is it you know
about me, European?"

"That you are the defender of the traditions of the Fashanti. That you have argued fiercely with those who would
try to modernize at any expense."

Masada Saku gave no reaction to this statement. But Sheriff knew the old man would remain impassive. He was looking at the sons, and in their eyes he discovered he had struck
truth.

"I'm hoping that's true," said Sheriff. "You've been able to hold off the rest because yours is the largest and wealthiest village in the tribe. If you were weak or without resources, they would have overthrown you. But you have maintained your principles and your position in spite of their opposition."

"Why do you find that so admirable?" Masada Saku was obviously leery of this—or any other—white man who came to his village dispensing lavish praise.

"Because, if you have maintained the traditions in other ways, perhaps you have also kept them in ways of war. Perhaps there are still warriors in your tribe."

"There *are* Fashanti warriors!" The exclamation broke from one of Masada Saku's sons. He leaped up from his squat on the floor and stood defiantly before Sheriff. The old man said impassively, "This is Tanata, my eldest son, my heir. There," Masada Saku said, pointing to the boy on the other side, "is my next eldest son, Limanti."

Sheriff nodded to each son. This was his opportunity to introduce himself. "I am Michael Sheriff." He was pleased with both Masada Saku's offspring, but particularly with Tanata. The young man's face was still screwed up with the intensity of his response to Sheriff's hope that Fashanti warriors still existed.

"Sit, Tanata," said the headman. The young man obeyed reluctantly, and with a scowl. "Yes, Mr. Sheriff," said Masada Saku, "there are still warriors in this village. We have kept a portion of our heritage intact. And we are capable of protecting ourselves, even now, in our weakened condition."

"Your sister's husband was not," said Sheriff.

Tanata's eyes widened at what he took to be an insult to his family.

Masada Saku said merely, "His village was small. He was outnumbered."

"The Kindu may soon outnumber you here, even in Fashata," said Sheriff. "They will certainly have weapons far superior to anything you can show. Because you're the largest town, you may be the last. But that means, Masada Saku, that when you fall, you will take all the Fashanti with you. Because when Fashata is no more, the Fashanti nation is no more."

"You would have us fight with them now?" Masada Saku asked.

"Soon," said Sheriff.

"What would you gain by this war?" Masada Saku then asked with every appearance of politeness. "Europeans do not promote tribal warfare without some gain in mind."

"Stability for Leikawa."

Tanata's laugh was derisive, but short. His father cut it off with a flare.

"Prince Motala vouches for you," said Masada Saku. "Would you lead the Fashanti into battle against the Kindu?"

"No," said Sheriff. The question was a trap, and he knew it. "No, I would only like the opportunity to fight alongside the Fashanti warriors."

"You are not a Fashanti warrior," said Masada Saku.

"Make me one."

Limanti, the second son, began blurting in the Fashanti tongue, gesticulating with his hands, but his father waved him down without even looking in his direction. "There is a way," said Masada Saku, "despite my son's objections. You are a male of another tribe, and there is a ritual . . ."

"The ritual requires a sponsor," Limanti said quickly, in English. "And no warrior of the Fashanti would take this white man—"

"I would," said Tanata, not even looking up. "I will sponsor this white man."

Masada Saku's face was impassive, but Sheriff thought he could detect a glint of pride in his eyes for the elder son's promise. The headman said, "The rite of initiation is difficult, Mr. Sheriff. Tests of the spirit as well as of the body. But if you are willing, and Tanata will be your guide . . ."

"I am willing," said Sheriff.

"If you succeed, you will join the Fashanti in their war against the Kindu," said Masada Saku.

"If I fail—" began Sheriff.

"You will!" exclaimed Limanti.

"If you fail," said Masada Saku, "we will go to war with the Kindu without your assistance."

Sheriff stood. "I will be honored to undergo the rites of the Fashanti warrior."

19

THE EARTH: Mother of us all.

To become a Fashanti warrior a man must be reborn. His previous life is chimera. The body must be taken back, back through the years and into the time before there was even a mind. Back to the earth out of which all life springs, and to which all life returns.

Stripped naked, Michael Sheriff was taken by the Fashanti warriors and led to the place where his life was to begin anew. In the bole of an enormous tree. Sheriff didn't recognize the species, but it stood alone—ancient and dark and brooding with enormous branches sweeping the ground in a large circle all around it—in a vast grassy plain. Beneath the canopy of dark green branches, on the bare earth, Michael Sheriff's body was smeared with brownish blue mud. The Fashanti men rubbed it into his hair, his skin, even into his crotch.

Then they layered furs over his body, old furs dyed the same brownish blue so that he couldn't tell the species of that either. The soft pelt side was turned to his own torso. There was a smoothness to the skins, an utter lack of tension. The skins covered him completely—only his mouth and nostrils were left free of the soft furs.

The feeling was not what he had expected—to be wrapped in furs in the middle of an African summer. But sheltered from the sun and hot dry wind by the great canopy of the tree, Sheriff was perfectly comfortable. He began to think that the sensation was one he remembered, and he puzzled over that.

Then he did remember.

He had once been submerged in a sensory-deprivation tank that was being used experimentally in one of the colleges near his home in Massachusetts. He recalled the way the professors had described the prenatal experience. It wasn't dissimilar from this. When the wrapping was completed, with double layers of fur pressed over his ears and eyes, Michael Sheriff's mouth was pried open, and a fistful of shelled nuts forced in.

He stiffened, for the nuts worked as a gag, hampering his breathing. A single bandage of fur was then wrapped across his mouth. Only his nostrils remained free. He forced relaxation into his lungs, and made the panic in his mind dissipate.

He was lifted and gently placed in a hollowed-out cavity in the bole of the tree.

He had noticed it before. Smooth on the inside. Dark. Man-sized.

If a man were closed up in the fetal position.

Michael Sheriff had no way of knowing whether the Fashanti warriors had gone away, or whether they were sitting in a circle watching him. Once the slight sensation of their lifting hands had been taken away he felt nothing. He saw nothing. Heard nothing.

He was suspended.

Floating.

But he couldn't move.

The furs were comfortable, but they were bondage.

When he tried to unlock his limbs he realized that his limbs must have been secured.

He tried to rock back and forth but could get no leverage with his feet. He couldn't feel that he was bracing against the wall of the tree on either side. It didn't even feel as if his muscles were working properly.

The nuts in his mouth were turning to acid by the action of his saliva.

He chewed them to get rid of the taste.

Boring. It was all going to be just boring. Wrapped up in the tree. He was supposed to be thinking about his rebirth. They had told him that much. Think about coming into manhood. Real manhood. Not the plasticized foolishness that most Americans experienced, but the bloody, gory manhood of a true Fashanti warrior.

Think about it.

Then the first wave hit. It was so intense he felt as if he'd been punched in the stomach. He should have expected it! He reeled inwardly and was furious with himself. The nuts. They were hallucinogenic.

The dreams would come.

They'd stifle his mind as his body was stifled with furs.

Another wave of intense sensation coursed through him. From the top of his head down to his feet. And then, finding no way out, it started back up again.

He wasn't going to have to think about rebirth.

It was going to come to him whether he liked it or not.

His adulthood was already slipping away.

His identity was being crowded out.

Sensation was exploding inside him.

He seemed to press outward against the stricture of the furs. But the furs remained a bondage. He still floated. No ground beneath him to hold him up. No walls to hold him in. No sky above to give him air to breathe. Just a nothingness beyond the pores of his skin.

Yet it was all comfortable.

That was the terrifying part. To be trapped in ecstasy. Bound in pleasure.

He ejaculated.

Or thought he did.

That part of his body was so far away.

Another country.

Another time.

Layers were peeled off. Whole layers. Deep abrasions scratched into his soul.

Pain. He wanted to feel pain. It was his defense, always.

A bullet in the arm. He tried to remember what it felt like. It was hot, sharp. He tried to remember the taste of his own blood. It was hot, sharp. If he hit somebody in the face, he could feel the cheekbone shatter. He tried to feel it on his knuckles. That jarring. To hear it in his ears. That crunch, dampened by flesh. He couldn't. He made fists and dug his fingernails into the palms of his hands. He wanted to feel pain. Wanted that trickle of blood down his wrist.

But the Fashanti had coated his hands and fingers with the mud, and his nails did no damage. It was like closing his hands over dough.

Comfortable.

Com—

It had all melted away.

Adulthood. Identity. Experience. Emotion.

Sensation alone was left, and it drove in waves. Beating out all that had been. Washing away all that had been known.

Until there was nothing left but his bondage.

Alone.

Smeared with mud. Wrapped in furs. Hidden in the bole of a tree that stood alone on the African plain.

He didn't know when it was done.

He had a vague sense of the chemicals seeping out of his body. Through sweat and piss.

For a single terrifying moment there was nothing— nothing at all.

Then the void was filled. Suddenly, as with seawater pouring into a hole dug in the beach.

The void was filled with courage. Self-reliance. Self-esteem.

There was no reason for them to be there.

What he had undergone was beyond humiliation. It was annihilation.

He still didn't know who he was.

But the courage, the self-reliance, and the self-esteem remained.

He slept.

When he waked, he was smiling.

The long-armed men of the Fashanti were bathing him in the river.

After what he'd seen in his mind, the blue of the sky and the green African vegetation seemed pale and washed-out.

Soon he was asleep again, in a tiny hut on the edge of the village. The distant night voices of the tribe seemed impossibly loud to him.

In the morning, he stumbled to his feet and then collapsed. He crawled round and round the hut till he was able to stand without falling.

Like a baby learning to walk, he thought.

Finally he could stand.

He remembered that his name was Michael Sheriff. That he lived in Massachusetts. That he had a son, and that his son's name was Roger.

He found food outside the hut. He ate ravenously.

Two days he stayed in the hut, alone, seeing no one, speaking to no one, learning the use of his limbs again. He had no idea how long he'd been in the bole of the tree.

On the morning of the third day, the tribesmen of the Fashanti appeared at the door of his hut. The birthing was done. Now it was time for the purification. This would not be the stuff of his head. This would be the test of his body.

"Are you ready?" he was asked.

"I am ready," he replied, in a hoarse, unnatural voice.

"Then give him to the women," said Masada Saku.

20

SHERIFF TRIED to cleanse his mind. First of the fear. Then of the humiliation. Then of the anger. *Try to make it an exercise. Think of it coolly, study it, analyze it, remember all you know about the Fashanti. Make believe you're an anthropologist.* He thought what all victims of torture tried to think of—the other side. The other side of whatever it was they were undergoing at that moment. When it ended.

Sheriff was spread-eagled, standing up, his limbs attached to a wooden frame with hemp. He was naked, his skin exposed to the sun. Around him danced a dozen Fashanti women, ceremonially made up, their faces covered with a bright blue clay pigment.

Their song was primitive, an ancient prayer to a god that Westerners had probably never heard of. They were nearly naked, their breasts exposed, some old and withering, but others full and upright, tempting in their firmness.

Each woman wielded a long narrow switch in her right hand.

They are going to cleanse me. That's all. They're just getting rid of the contaminations.

Every culture did it. But that wasn't much of a consolation.

The song they sang was no longer a prayer. It was now directed toward Sheriff, not to the god, and it was derisive. The circle they formed tightened around him. Each revolution brought the women closer. Soon there was an occa-

sional blow as a switch reached out and sliced at his body.
He clenched his teeth, knowing that the Fashanti warriors
who stood at a distance would consider the cries of a man at
a woman's hand to be beneath contempt.

More women came within striking distance. Their
song picked up in intensity and volume. They were en-
joying their role in the making of a Fashanti warrior.
Sheriff's body was soon under constant assault. The little
cuts of the switches, deceptively thin and slight, were
added and then compounded until the pain became wave-
like and unending.

Tiny rivulets of blood sprang from Sheriff's body. On his
back, his stomach, his buttocks, the cuts sliced through his
skin and brought forth the red liquid as plentifully as his
sweat. Dozen upon dozen the blows rained down on him,
and the contemptuous song of the Fashanti women rang
shrilly in his ears. Finally, Michael Sheriff's body responded with unconscious jerks when one blow landed on a
place that was suddenly endowed with an unnatural
sensitivity—beneath his arms, on the inside of his thigh, or
some spot that had been lashed one time too often.

The women's faces became more intense as their attacks
were delivered at close quarters. Their singing grew louder,
gaining an element of sexuality. Too, some hint of a personal revenge that each female was delivering—slight recompense for a lifetime of blows at the hand of a jungle fate.
The thin lengths of wood swept through the afternoon air ferociously. The torture—that incalculable accumulation of an
infinity of tiny pains—made Sheriff's entire body a closed,
sensate vehicle of agony.

It was, he knew, much worse than some masculine flog-
ging. That a man could take with ferocious determination.
Ten strokes of a bull were, in the end, only ten strokes.
Maybe one of them could break a limb, but they were of a
finite number. A man could pace them, brace for the beginning, and look forward to the ending. Not this ongoing as-
semblage of stings that could never be counted, this

accretion of pain that could never be gauged. It was like being stung in a world that held nothing but wasps.

What has hurt this bad? he asked himself in a part of his brain that still heard the women's singing. He was searching for a thought that would occupy more of his mind. Think, think, and each thought would crowd out one single tiny blow of pain. The women searched out his tenderness. Who had ever paid such attention to the back of his calves? They were digging gullies between his ribs, and each gully ran blood. The switches tangled in his pubic hair, and pulled it out strand by strand. *What has hurt this bad?*

In Vietnam. There had been a landmine. He had stepped on a dud but his friend Bill Franklin hadn't been so lucky. The thing exploded, sending deadly shrapnel through the air, slicing Bill into a dozen pieces and embedding itself it Sheriff's own body. He had had to stay silent and still for nine hours, smelling the scraps of his best buddy as they rotted in the jungle air, while Viet Cong had patrolled all around him. Unable to speak, terrified of falling asleep, Sheriff had maintained his consciousness and his sanity and he had waited it out for the American troops he was not even sure were in the area. That had been the worst. *Think about that,* he demanded of himself as his mouth flew open once more when a switch sliced perfectly into the tender hollow of his left ear.

His mouth opened, finally, in utter suffering. But he shut it, and did not cry out. This was only the beginning of his trial. He would not give in before the Fashanti.

Then all at once it stopped. The blows and the singing together. A sudden absence of sensation as wrenching as the pain itself had been. He thought he'd passed out. He didn't even know if his eyes were opened or closed. If he were standing upright or was flat on his back. Nothing registered.

His eyes had been closed, for after a while they opened and he saw Tanata standing before him. Impassive. Masada Saku's son wasn't going to congratulate Sheriff for having his body cleansed by a pack of women. That was just a warmup.

A knife appeared in Tanata's hand. He cut the binding ropes and Sheriff had to use all his strength not to collapse. He had stood naked, spread-eagled for two hours before the ceremony had begun. His body had to be displayed to the gods before the Fashanti were allowed to test him. If Sheriff had given in to sunstroke, a very real possibility, then the gods would have spoken their displeasure. He would have been exiled from Fashata immediately. But the gods at least were allowing the test. So the women had begun their ritual. And now, Sheriff knew, the men would take over.

The facing parallel lines of Fashanti warriors before him made the second part of the ritual obvious. The gauntlet—a recurrent rite in primitive civilizations, and many civilizations that were not so very primitive at all. Tanata gave Sheriff a beaten metal shield about a meter in diameter. Sheriff's right hand slipped weakly through the straps of lion sinew.

He tried to pull himself together with the thought that he *had* to. He flexed his muscles, forcing blood through the veins that had been cut off by the bondage. He moved his knees and demanded that they become supple again. In a real battle, adrenaline would have forged its way through his body. He had to press that interior drug into service now. His ability to bring himself back to fighting shape almost instantly was part of what was being tested now. Tribal warfare, the Fashanti knew, didn't allow much in the line of respites.

Tanata nodded again. It was time. Sheriff studied the two rows of men. The first man on his right held a spear capable of delivering instant death. The man on his left, though, held only a bludgeon. The point was obvious. To survive—to win—the probationary warrior had to endure a mammoth blow of the club in order to fend off a slighter stroke of the sword. But the clubbing only bruised the muscle—it didn't kill. The sword stroke didn't hurt as much—but you died.

It was surprising how many chose the stroke of the sword, simply from fear of the massive bludgeon.

Sheriff approached. His body tight, his eyes fixed on the man with the spear. He began to move. The man with the spear shook his head—*no, no* with quick motions. Sheriff was puzzled, then he understood. Tanata had run to the other side of the gauntlet. Sheriff's success was as much a matter of Tanata's honor as the white man's own pride. To urge him on Tanata would stand at the terminus of the gauntlet and wait. His presence there would be a motivation for his protégé to succeed.

All right, Sheriff said to himself, *I understand.* A man could allow himself to die for many reasons. Soldiers often gave in when it was only a question of their own survival. But the Fashanti understood that a man who owed another man honor would fight beyond endurance. That was another part of the test here. The Fashanti were telling Sheriff that he could give up. He could break down. But if he did he would have to look into the eyes of Tanata, who had himself risked disgrace by venturing to sponsor a European in the rites of the Fashanti warrior.

Sheriff approached the line. The first two warriors prepared themselves. Strange, thought Sheriff, I'm walking into a sucker punch. The warriors' arms tensed. Sheriff moved. It was a quick and effective maneuver on his part. The motion was so fast and unexpected that the two Fashanti didn't get in the licks they thought they would. The bludgeon glanced off Sheriff's shoulder, hurting like hell, but not nearly as badly as it would have if the man had been more prepared.

The spear was easily deflected off Sheriff's shield. The second pair of warriors were just as surprised, and not at all quick to react. Not only did Sheriff escape the second spear, he was able to move efficiently enough that the second club-wielding warrior got in no blow at all. His club struck the ground behind Sheriff's lifted foot.

At the end of the line Tanata allowed a tiny tight smile that quickly evaporated. It was almost a taunt, and it certainly had that effect. For it threw Michael Sheriff off balance. The spear-carrier was deflected again, but this time the club-wielder had figured out the rhythm of Sheriff's feinting. The heavy wooden mallet fell between Sheriff's shoulders, where his back still smarted from the stinging blows of the Fashanti women.

Waves of pain poured through his body, crashing in his feet and in his brain till he was staggering forward.

Forward to the next pair.

His shield went up automatically. If it hadn't, his right arm would have been sliced off.

But he had to take the blow of the third club-man. In the small of his back.

He lurched forward.

He saw Tanata's face through a veil of his perspiration. Or tears. He didn't know why he didn't fall. His head seemed only inches above the bleached earth. His legs and feet, propelling him forward, seemed lost somewhere far behind him. How could a man keep his balance? And ward off fatal blows from his right with only a thin metal shield? And sustain blows from his left, from one club that was heavier than the last? He didn't breathe. He didn't think. He lifted his chin, hoping to see Tanata. Tanata to pull him on toward the end. The end of the gauntlet. The end of pain.

But it wasn't Tanata he saw there.

It was Roger.

Beckoning him on with a small smile of pride.

Sheriff went on, stumbling forward between the last two Fashanti warriors.

The last two were always the worst.

With Roger's smile to succor him, Michael Sheriff lurched to the right, pushing up under the blow of the sword. In so doing, he avoided the blow of the club altogether.

His balance gave way at last, as it ought to have years before. He tumbled at the feet of his son.

Not his son. Roger's feet weren't black.

It was Tanata again. Tanata raised Michael Sheriff up, and declared him a warrior of the Fashanti.

... *21*

ROGER JOGGED alone through the woods of Massachusetts, the sweat pouring off him. He'd had only a few days with his father, but it seemed as if a hundred important patterns had been set in that short time. Now that his father was gone, the patterns all seemed sadly incomplete.

On this run every morning through the deep forest that lay within the compound of Michael Sheriff's property, Roger thought about his father, and about what he had discovered on his trip east.

Not what he had expected, that was certain.

Now it was hard to remember just what he had thought he'd find when he arrived, after ten years of dreaming about his father, of wondering what it would be like to be with him and at his side. Ten years of wishing, and speculating, and imagining.

He'd had vague ideas of Michael Sheriff owning a small house somewhere near Boston, with neighbors close in on every side, and a fence that separated the tired lawn from a Burger King parking lot, and maybe a couch where Roger could sleep. Michael Sheriff would have some fancy-schmancy job downtown that was boring as hell but brought in lots of money.

That reality would have satisfied Roger, so anxious had he been to get out of Nevada. And away from his mother. Hard to believe she'd ever been married to Michael Sheriff. Hard to believe—

Hard to believe what he'd found when he arrived.

Even the area was different from what he's expected. He'd never been east. He thought that Massachusetts was like Nevada, except cold and wet. It was totally different. Massachusetts was *old*. Lived in. Roger always felt that he was walking over land that was saturated with the bones of the people who had lived there before. When people in Nevada talked about an old house, they meant one that had been built in the nineteen-fifties. When people in Massachusetts said they lived in an old house, they meant that Paul Revere had ridden past it. Massachusetts wasn't just wet, it was lush. The forest in Sudbury was green and dense and the ground was uneven with the carcasses of thousands of trees that had grown up and died and fallen over and rotted. Birds nested everywhere. The East was supposed to be densely populated, but Roger saw more wildlife from his bedroom window than he'd seen in a decade in Nevada. It just wasn't what he'd imagined.

Neither was his father.

Roger had wanted—and wanted desperately—to be with Michael Sheriff. But he'd somehow expected the man to be like the fathers of his friends. Browbeaten by life, if not by their lives. Worn down. Cagey. Dispirited. Roger was so desperate for direction in his life that he would have gladly taken even such a man as that.

But Michael Sheriff was such a man as Roger had not dared hope to find. Uncompromising. Sure in his physical manner, sure in his careful speech, sure in every gesture. Roger thought he had figured out what made his father different.

Michael Sheriff had control over his life. That's what it seemed to Roger. He could hardly believe it. Simply because he'd never come across it before. But his father was proof that such control could and did exist. And if his father had it, then Roger could too.

Of course Roger didn't yet know everything about his father there was to know. Not by a long shot. Michael Sheriff didn't go to work every day. But he owned a spread that was impressive even to a boy used to the cheap wastelands of

Nevada. He had a big house, and Roger could see that it hadn't been fixed up out of Montgomery Ward and Sears. He had a housekeeper and a groundsman, and Roger never once saw his father give a second thought to what a thing cost. It was as if money had no meaning for him.

But that business was not as strange as what had happened at Andy's Surplus. That seemed a dream now, too. Like Nevada. It was hard to believe that it happened. That he saw four people killed. That he saw *his father* shoot a woman in the breast with a machine gun. That the woman had died, strangled in her own blood not ten feet away from him. That nobody got arrested. And that nobody appeared to feel guilty about what they'd done, or seemed to take the incident as anything but a matter of course.

It was what happened when you went out to buy underwear, that's all. Sometimes people got killed.

Roger never really talked to his father about that. Hadn't asked questions. Oh, he'd wanted to, all right. Wanted to ask those questions one after the other. But Roger knew that his father wouldn't have answered them with full truthfulness. So Roger had decided to keep quiet. If he didn't ask questions, maybe he wouldn't be lied to. And if his vision and his understanding didn't get clouded up with lies, then maybe he'd be able to figure out the truth.

He was working on that now. Working on that harder than he was working on the running. And the sit-ups. And the pectorals that his father told him were "only adequate." Here's what he'd figured out so far: Michael Sheriff worked for the Chairman. He did what the Chairman told him to do. What he did was dangerous, and had always been dangerous. He was obviously good at it because he was still alive to run alongside Roger through the Massachusetts forest. Roger also knew that Katrina wasn't a real housekeeper. She did the work, but Roger always had the feeling that her soul was elsewhere. Katrina had that same hardness of eye that Roger detected in the Chairman. And sometimes had detected in his father. A hundred much smaller details about his father's life Roger had figured out as well, just by keeping his eyes and his ears open. He treasured them up. He made them into a dossier in his mind. The time would come when the file would be complete.

Almost complete.

Roger had the feeling that nobody would ever know the whole of Michael Sheriff.

He did the exercises that allowed him to fill his lungs with air. The sweat cooled on his body. He was overtaken with light-headedness when he came into the shadow of his father's house, but in a few moments that passed too. He was getting used to this regimen. It wasn't because he was taking shortcuts either. He was just doing it right, and doing it right got simpler and simpler. Oh God, if only the rest of his life could be like this morning run. That easy to figure out, that simple to *do*.

But it wouldn't be.

He knew that. He was just marking time till his father came back, and told him what to do.

Anything Michael Sheriff set up as a plan wasn't going to be easy.

Not as easy as finishing up in that factory called a high school in Nevada. Not as easy as driving up and down that blacktop strip, drinking beer one night, gambling quarters another night, screwing a girl in the back of her Camaro on a third night, and doing all three on the weekend. Not as easy as finding some asshole job on the asphalt strip that kept the car running, kept the beer flowing, kept the girls hot in the back seat of the Camaro. He could be dumb and poor if he got legal work—running a gas station late nights. He could be really dumb and pretty well-off if he got illegal work—running coke in and out of old Lester's place out on 212. But where would all that have gotten him by the time he was thirty? He'd have a life that was a great big giant sleeping pill.

He'd seen it happen. It had already started to happen to him when he finally packed it all in and came east. All the way across the country he'd kept his foot on the accelerator, praying hard that his father was the kind of man to keep him out of that shit.

Michael Sheriff was that kind of man.

Roger's father hadn't lived that kind of life. Not to get where he was today. Roger found himself wondering about that, though. Michael Sheriff was thirty-eight. What had happened in the twenty years that had passed since he was Roger's age? Roger's mother had told him nothing about Michael Sheriff. She didn't like to talk about him. Roger wondered if he'd ever find out the real story. He doubted if his father himself would ever come forward with that information.

After he showered and changed, he came downstairs to breakfast. It was one of Katrina's days off, but she had set up the automatic coffee pot for him the night before, and it was waiting for him now. He poured a cup and carried it into the dining room. He'd drink that and then see about rustling up something more substantial.

But that wasn't what happened that morning.

For on the table, beside Roger's place, were two thick manila envelopes with steel and string clasps. They looked as if they'd been pulled straight out of someone's filing cabinet.

Roger was certain they hadn't been there the night before when he'd gone to bed. Katrina had been off since the previous morning. The groundsman stayed on the gate, or worked in the gardens. Roger had never seen him inside the house.

But here the envelopes were. On them were tapes bearing the simple legend:

SHERIFF, M

THE SHIELD

. . . 22

TANATA AND MICHAEL SHERIFF ran across the savannah beneath a star-bright, moonless sky. Each man wore only a loincloth; each carried a shield in his left hand, and a spear in his right.

Sheriff had always been in good shape. Of course. It came with the job. But the last three weeks had tested his body in a way that it had never been tested before. And to an extent he couldn't remember since his first week at Marine boot camp. He got through it now the way he got through it then. He didn't resist. He had merged his mind into the Fashanti mentality—just as so many years before, he had given himself up to his drill instructor, sadistic insane bastard though the man had been. The body business had come afterward—when you had given over your mind and your will—the body dragged after as a matter of course. This wasn't the time and place to be doing a set of suburban exercises. Five years on a Nautilus machine wasn't going to prepare you for a barefoot run across untrammeled African savannah. And the Fashanti weren't preparing themselves for a corporate softball game. They were going to war. Against an enemy that killed even without provocation.

Sheriff's feet had finally toughened enough to tolerate the open running on the savannah with only a covering of skin. But he knew that it would only undercut Tanata's trust in him—and the others' grudging respect—if he even once showed himself to be just another soft European. His first mile run had hurt as much as the bruises and

145

welts of his initiation, but the bottoms of his feet were practically horn now.

Sheriff and Tanata ran past a herd of gazelle trustfully grazing on the tall grass. *This is what Roger should know about,* Sheriff thought. Jogging a few miles through the tame forests of Massachusetts forests wasn't the stuff of manhood. It just staved off middle-class spread.

Others might come into a situation like Leikawa's with helicopters and sophisticated explosives and blow the enemy to pieces. That worked when you wanted to get rid of an army. But it didn't restore a people's self-respect. That was a part of what this mission was all about. The Fashanti had to rediscover the part of themselves that only Masada Saku's few warriors had retained in secret. That meant increasing the preparedness of the men of Fashanti, and igniting the dormant pride of the tribe's military heritage.

The two men raced farther and faster across the savannah. Tanata had proved to be a good companion and better friend. Sheriff had grown to respect and admire the young man. They spent their days hunting or drilling the young Fashanti warriors. To fill out the ranks of this tribal army, they trained youngsters ahead of their time, and recalled a number of the older men to their former status as warriors.

But tonight, it was only Tanata and Sheriff, scouting out the nearest Kindu encampment, the semipermanent camp from which the Kindu executed their raids on the mines.

It seemed appropriate to Sheriff that he was dressed this way. Wearing only a loincloth, and that not for the sake of modesty, but to keep his genitals out of the way as he ran. Nakedness would have been as distracting as white tie and tails. He was painted blue, a darker shade than the Fashanti usually wore, because Sheriff's skin was far whiter than theirs. In a part of the world where the nearest streetlamp was five hundred miles distant, and the Milky Way appeared as it must have to the men who raised Stonehenge and the Carnac stones, starlight was an illumination to be reckoned with. Wasn't it the ancient Celts who had painted themselves blue? Sheriff tried to remember.

In any case, the Fashanti had gone those ancient warriors one better. The Irish hadn't mixed in animal grease with their pigments, so far as he knew, so that they stank as fiercely as they looked. The Fashanti, as a tribe and people, possessed a highly developed sense of smell. This was one of the few facts about Leikawa that MIS had not prepared Michael Sheriff for. They took advantage of this by giving their warriors a light covering of oil that was extracted from the entrails of a particular kind of hyena that scavanged in the vicinity. The hyenas were hunted for that one purpose. The Fashanti could recognize one another by this scent—and more important, they could recognize the enemy purely by the fact they had no coating of the hyena oil.

Away from exhaust fumes, tobacco smoke, and the other thousand industrial scents to which modern Western man is subjected every day, Sheriff found his sense of smell sharpened almost beyond his capacity to endure it. He could easily identify most of the men of the tribe merely by their odor. He could walk around the village with his eyes closed and know it like a map, for every hut had a distinctive smell. He knew when something had died in the forest a hundred yards from his dwelling, and he even packed away his cherished Sobranies, for the taste had grown overpowering.

His body moved with a fluidity he hadn't felt in ages. Years of testing himself against iron and running for pleasure had led him to forget the extent to which those things were artificial—as arbitrary as employing seconds to measure the terms of a man's life, or a yardstick to gauge the distance from the earth to the sun. He forgot five-mile goals, and five-minute tests. He ran harder than he'd ever run before, not to get a certain distance under a certain time—but because he had to get somewhere, and if he didn't go it quick enough he might just die.

He no longer seemed to have emotions. Only motives.

Goads sharp as the pointed sticks with which Fashanti boys hunted the hyenas. Loyalty to Masada Saku and his eldest son Tanata. Vengeance for the ignominious deaths so many of the Fashanti had suffered at the hands of the Kindu. Preservation of a way of life that was now a part of himself.

He didn't think of MIS, or the Chairman, or any portion of his mission except as it related to the destruction of the Kindu. He wasn't a representative of the United Nations pushing for stability in a troubled region. He was a Fashanti warrior, painted blue and smelling of hyena, running through the starlit night with the single intention of murdering as many Kindu as he could before dawn.

They moved stealthily around the Kindu camp. Leaving their spears in the tall grass, they were armed only with knives. They had crossed the savannah with two motives in mind. Sheriff wanted information on the number of the Kindu, on their weapons, and—if possible—on the three Europeans believed to be in league with the tribe. Tanata wanted revenge for the killing of the headman, the husband of his father's sister.

Tanata slept with the old man's skull at his pillow. It would remain on the ground until his murder was avenged. Only then would it be raised to the shelf of honor above Masada Saku's door.

As a form of politeness, Sheriff gave Tanata the first death: the outermost sentinel.

Sheriff watched in surprise as Tanata used one of the moves he himself had learned in Marine basic training.

The human brain is a vulnerable organ. A coiled mass of gray-red mush. It's given a rigid casing of bone for protection, and the skull *is* hard, but it has its weak points.

Tanata was silent as he moved toward the Kindu. As soon as he was within striking distance, he leaped. His hand was smashed, palm out, into the Kindu's face, breaking the man's nose and forcing the shattered bone up into the center of the skull, deep into the brain. All of a sudden, there was nothing.

The whole sequence took no more than five seconds. Tanata didn't even bother to check that the man was dead before he arranged the corpse. He didn't need to, Sheriff knew. Tanata would have felt death in his hand.

The two Fashanti warriors—one of them white beneath his blue paint—continued their prowl around the quiet Kindu camp. Sheriff's knife took out the next sentinel they found. One quiet, quick, and earnest cut of the blade sliced open the man's throat. Sheriff held his hand there one second to hold back any possible scream. He turned the man a foot to the left so that the blood spewed silently on dry, matted grass. Then he pushed the dying man facedown so that he covered the pool of his own blood, preventing the stink of it from rising on the late night wind.

As Tanata had with the first sentinel, Michael Sheriff squatted beside the dead man. With a finger dipped in the dead man's blood, he traced the Fashanti ideogram for war on the corpse's bare back.

Revenge wasn't complete without that symbol. It showed that the vengeance had transpired in a straightforward, deliberate manner.

The symbol would also serve as a warning to the Kindu. It would plant the first seeds of fear in the soul of the tribe that had known no enemies for a long time.

Two more sentinels, and they went together with Sheriff and Tanata's knives slashing in unison.

Sheriff found the shed in which the Kindu arms were stored. AK-47s. That suggested Russian backing all right, but was by no means conclusive proof of Soviet involvement.

Anybody could get AK-47s these days. Just as anybody could get M16s. And Israeli Uzis. Often, for an insurgent group, the question of which weapon to buy was based on such considerations as the cheapness of the ammunition, or already established stockpiles of spare parts. The weapons themselves were no difficulty. Anybody could get anything.

And in the corner of the shed, grenade launchers and grenades.

For a few minutes, Sheriff dropped out of his Fashanti mind. He was CIA-trained Michael Sheriff once more. Just for a few minutes. Long enough to spirit out two of the launchers and a dozen of the grenades. And to set up the launchers fifty yards away in the savannah grass.

Tanata sat with his back to Sheriff, facing toward the distant Fashanti town from which they'd come, as if none of this modern warfare business had anything to do with him.

It was nearing dawn, but the grenades streaked westward, toward a sky that was still black with night. That's where the explosions were, too.

First the ammunition shed.

It blew up very bright and very orange against the dark sky. The dry savannah grass also began to burn. The explosions came one after the other, out of that single shed, as different stores ignited.

While that was going on, Sheriff launched more grenades into the midst of the Kindu warriors who had run shouting and confused out of their huts.

Sheriff had decided to launch an even dozen grenades. After that the Kindu should have been able to pinpoint his location.

Exactly what they did. But by the time they got to the grenade launchers in the beaten-down grass, Michael Sheriff was gone.

He and Tanata were sprinting back toward Fashata, as if running a race with the dawn at their backs.

When they reached the village, and the headman demanded a report, Tanata reported to his father only that they had killed four Kindu—the four Kindu on which they had painted the ideogram for war.

The twenty or so Kindu that Sheriff's grenades had cut up past putting back together again didn't count.

Sheriff made no protest, but he reflected that this was the first body count he'd ever known that was *down*graded.

That morning, Masada Saku raised the skull of his sister's husband from the earth to the shelf above his door. From that vantage, the dead headman's sightless eyes blessed all those who departed that house for war against the Kindu.

23

He SAT in his father's favorite leather chair and put his legs on the matching ottoman. Each manila envelope contained several hundred pages. He opened the one that had been placed on top, pulled out the sheets, and leafed through them. Each page had been photocopied from a variety of originals. The photocopying gave them a deceptive innocuous similarity.

With a deep breath he began to read. He didn't stop until the middle of the afternoon. By the time he finished the last page his hands were shaking. A sour stench came from his underarms. He hadn't eaten since six o'clock the previous evening but the last thing on his mind was food. There'd be no sit-ups this afternoon.

He didn't hear Katrina come in, but suddenly she was there, coming through the dining room with sandwiches on a tray. He must have eaten them because later he saw that the plate with crumbs was left on the floor beside the chair. He looked at the residue in the glass there, and realized that he must have drunk milk. He didn't remember it.

He took the pages and carefully put them back in the envelopes. He placed the envelopes back on the dining room table where he'd found them. He went to his room, took off his clothes, lay down on his bed, and stared at the ceiling. After a few minutes he got up and closed the window. Drew the yellow shade. Pulled the curtains closed. Lay down again and looked back up to the ceiling.

Michael Sheriff. Code Name: The Shield.

That had been the simple typed heading at the top of each sheet. To facilitate filing. To categorize the surreal.

The pages had been in some sort of order, for information was clustered, but Roger hadn't been able to make out much more than that. He'd read all the pages through—at least those that were in English and Spanish—and he'd pieced the picture together himself.

The picture of his father.

Not the kind of picture you put in a silver frame and propped up on your dresser when you went away to college. A different kind altogether.

Michael Sheriff, Roger's father, had lived a fairly normal life. An all-American life, at least the first seventeen years of it. He grew up in midstate Illinois in a happy and productive family of farmers. Roger's grandfather had grown corn, then switched to soybeans. How strange, Roger thought, never to have known even as much as that . . .

Michael Sheriff had been one of three sons. Had worked on the farm while receiving fine grades in high school.

Two report cards to the photocopied page.

Michael Sheriff's two elder brothers had been his idols, and they were the same sort of hardworking scholar/farmers that Michael himself was.

Until they were murdered.

My uncles.

Ralph was a year older than Michael, Tom two years older. Both studying at Illinois-Urbana, majoring in animal husbandry. They clearly intended to return to the farm. Their father was saving to buy more acreage.

During the summer of Michael Sheriff's seventeenth year, Ralph and Tom were home from college. One Friday night in July the two older brothers borrowed their father's old Plymouth and went to the drive-in with a pair of sisters that they had gone to high school with. Afterward they had taken the girls parking on a back road of a nearby state park.

The day before three men had escaped from the maximum-security prison at Joliet. But Joliet was eighty-five miles away and nobody expected to find the men down here.

Yet that night the three escapees did turn up, on the back road of a state park that nobody ever went to.

It was never clear what exactly had happened.

Whether the convicts were simply depraved. Whether they had been provoked by the Sheriff boys. Whether the Sheriff boys had resisted being taken hostage and had tried to prevent the sisters from being raped.

It was never clear what exactly had happened, because both couples died. The two women were repeatedly raped, then stabbed. Sexual intercourse occurred again, after death.

Ralph and Tom were tied to trees, so it seems likely that they were made to watch.

Afterward, their throats were cut.

It was Michael who found them, for he and his brothers had occasionally fished at the park. Once he got to the park, the carrion birds led young Michael Sheriff to the four corpses.

He shot the crows that were perched on his brothers' shoulders, tearing the flesh from their sightless faces.

The next day he'd picked up the call on his father's shortwave radio—the three convicts had been sighted by another farmer. They were digging potatoes out of a field, and devouring them then and there. The police were on their way, but seventeen-year-old Michael Sheriff got there first. With the same gun, Michael Sheriff shot the three convicts who had killed his brothers.

The district attorney of the county was in an awkward position. Three men were dead, and there was a minor who admitted to the killings. In the opinion of everyone in town, justice had been done when the escaped convicts were shot. But it wouldn't do to have the boy walk the streets—that would show a civic contempt for the law and the Constitution. But to throw the boy in jail for what he ought to be given a medal for—

The district attorney met with the lawyer that Michael's father had hired. The two of them went to the local judge, and the three of them agreed—there would be no prosecution if Michael Sheriff joined the army.

Seventeen-year-old Michael Sheriff refused.
He'd already been accepted into the marines.

Roger had read on.

He absorbed his father's service record in a state somewhere between awe and horror. He couldn't escape the obvious conclusion—Michael Sheriff was a born killer. Never without cause. Never without justification. Nor were his targets ever innocents or civilians. But in battle Michael Sheriff had turned himself into a killing machine that stunned even the marines with its cold efficiency.

Except machines don't have luck or guardian angels or higher powers looking over them, and it seemed that Michael Sheriff did. Mines exploded within a few yards of him—killing the ARVN unit that had captured him. He broke his arm—and was kept from taking part in an ambush that backfired. And so on, incidents repeated a hundred times with the same chorus: *that lucky bastard.*

He came through with scars and medals. You saw the scars when he took off his clothes. Nobody ever saw the medals. The last two of Sheriff's five years in Vietnam were spent undercover. His actual commission—he had risen to the rank of lieutenant colonel on account of battlefield heroism—was with the marines. But his new boss was the CIA. He was effective and efficient. Michael Sheriff studied torture the way that Roger had once studied Chevy engines. Roger read with a feverish queasiness a report that his father had written on the steps—one through six—by which any member of the Viet Cong could be made to give up a secret. Roger didn't doubt that the method worked. Roger decided that he would have given up halfway through the first level.

After the war, Michael Sheriff was a cop for nine months. Busted for insubordination; that is, for refusing to accept the bribes his superiors were accepting. Took employment with five different private agencies, all with long names that gave no information except that they dealt with security. A police record began to form here: arrests for break-ins, for assaults, complaints for denial of civil rights, a number of arrests. But no prosecutions. Not a single day spent in jail.

All that said something, but Roger wasn't sure exactly what. Maybe that his father had remained in the employ of the CIA. Who ever heard of a CIA man who went to jail for anything?

Then formal notice of his termination of employment with the CIA.

That must have been when he joined MIS, Roger surmised. But of MIS, of the Chairman, of any of the exploits of The Shield, there was no notice. Those items had been kept out of the envelopes that Roger was given. The missions of MIS were secret, it appeared, in a way that the classified exploits of the CIA were not. But even if the records didn't include his father's most recent work in the line, there was still plenty to occupy Roger's attention.

Because Roger himself had begun to figure in his father's files.

He had gone cold, reading that first piece of paper with his name on it. He'd only been two years old, and Michael Sheriff had demanded leave to see him.

Other references too, many of them. Even a typewritten list of Roger's third-grade friends, with their addresses, and some penciled annotations concerning their parents. Great Christ! There were names on that list that Roger didn't even remember now.

A catalog of the houses where he'd lived with his mother. A list of men his mother had gone to bed with.

It was longer than even Roger had imagined.

More requests for leave.

Roger remembered a camping trip his father had taken him on when he was in the sixth grade. It was supposed to last a week. It lasted three days. His father was called away. Now Roger discovered why. He found out that his father had packed up his tent, hugged Roger good-bye at his mother's front door, and gone off to Mexico and shot sixteen men dead the following morning.

More surveillance reports on his mother. The bars she went to sober, and the motel rooms she ended up in, drunk.

Surveillance reports on Roger himself. Drinking at age thirteen. Smoking dope at fourteen. Selling dope at sixteen. *Christ,* he sweated. *His father had known.*

That brought Roger up on the bed with a start in his darkened room. His father *hadn't* known. That little piece of confession had come as a very unhappy surprise to Michael Sheriff in Big Sam's place—Roger had seen the pain in his father's eyes. Therefore Michael Sheriff hadn't seen these files. If that was true, then why the fuck had they been put in a place where Roger was sure to see them?

Why the fuck?

24

MICHAEL SHERIFF SAT just outside the circle of huts that marked the perimeter of Fashata. He still wore only his loincloth. A residue of blue paint still stained his body. His feet were in such condition that he might have wondered if he'd ever wear shoes again. Except that he did not think now beyond the limits of any other Fashanti warrior. If Tanata and his father Masada Saku did not think about shoes, why should he?

The events of the past days rambled through his mind. He closed his eyes as he recounted them. Michael Sheriff had killed many times before. Legally, as a soldier in Vietnam, as a policeman. Illegally, for the CIA and MIS. Most of the deaths he'd caused were forgotten—if you'd shot a dozen snipers from a distance of a hundred yards over a period of three years, you couldn't be expected to distinguish them in your memory. Except maybe the one whose foot got caught in a limb of the tree he'd been hiding in, and who was caught upside down, hanging a few feet above the ground—and whose head was used for a few minutes' target practice by the other guys in the platoon. Him you remembered, but not the others. Deaths were like scabs. You tried not to let your memory pick at them.

But these most recent killings? His eyes remained closed. This mission seemed different from the others. He felt it had touched his soul. One by one the layers of what others called civilization had been torn from him. Now, nearly naked, painted blue, and stinking of hyena oil, he sat and heard the piping, primeval music of Fashanti women. Now singing praise for the returning victorious. Now lamenting over the dead who would never return to the beds of their wives.

He snorted—a little derision directed at himself. Where was he two months ago, the sophisticated world traveler? He had been in the bar of the Georges V in Paris, sipping Glenfiddich and wondering if he'd have to get up to seduce the woman at the next table—or could he do it entirely with his eyes? That's where he'd been two months ago.

Since he'd come to live with the Fashanti he hadn't tasted alcohol. Hadn't seen a white woman. Hadn't heard the ringing of a telephone. Hadn't smelled the exhaust of a gasoline engine. When a jet flew over—this was rare, for the Fashanti even lived outside of air-traffic lanes—Sheriff found himself staring upward in openmouthed wonder.

The sophisticated world traveler. The man about town. The computer-age operative for the ultimate computer-age organization.

Gaping at a twin-engine jet.

Once a day, he had to remind himself of his identity and his mission. Just so he wouldn't forget it. He was Michael Sheriff, The Shield. By employing the Fashanti to overwhelm and defeat the Kindu, he would defuse the Leikawan time bomb. He was erasing the headlines in the papers a year hence, the headlines that talked of a bloody revolution in Leikawa, of official corruption, of the discovery of outback slavery, of Soviet and Eastern bloc support of insurgents, of the misery of the people of Leikawa, and the total destruction of the admirable tribe of the Fashanti—and the editorials which cried, "Why didn't someone do something to keep this from happening?"

Because if Michael Sheriff, The Shield, did not help the Fashanti to defeat the Kindu now, that's exactly what *would* appear in the papers a year from now. He had to make the preventive incision now. Cut out the Kindu. Break their power. And in so doing, give the Fashanti a chance to regain their self-respect, and to reestablish their ability to protect themselves.

But at what cost to the man who was The Shield would all this be accomplished—if he *could* accomplish it? That was Sheriff's question now. How often could he descend to this level and bring himself back up? He'd done it before of course. Numerous times. Been in situations like this—not painted blue in a loincloth, but the equivalent—and the following week he'd been standing at the gaming tables of Monte Carlo. Seducing an unsuspecting Soviet agent at a financiers' party in Rome the week after that.

But how often could he make these switches? Turn off. Turn on.

His hands massaged his thighs, bulged with muscle after the incredible amount of running he'd done in the past two months. How often could he leave a situation like this and go back to the wheel of his Volvo? Back to his house? Back to . . .

His son.

There was something about Roger mixed in with his feelings about this whole episode. Why, he wondered? He found Roger slipping often into his mind. Sometimes he would think that Roger would enjoy this life, learning the ancient wisdom of the Fashanti. Certainly Roger could have benefited from passing the rites of a warrior that the Fashanti had forced Michael to endure. Any male would have toughened from that, and from the preparations necessary to endure it at all.

Other times Sheriff wondered if he wanted Roger to experience *any* of it. Why should any man have to come to places like this godforsaken corner of Africa and risk his life every day? Every hour of every day? Sheriff had always answered that question by himself, for himself. Someone had to do it, it might as well be he. But that rationalization didn't work when it came to his son, Roger.

There were a thousand reasons it shouldn't be Roger.

At the same time that Sheriff wanted Roger hardened into a man, he wanted to protect the boy. To keep him from having to learn what Michael had learned. There were times that Michael Sheriff felt he had spent the last twenty years of his life slogging through a world of scum. Was it right for him to wave back over his shoulder and shout, ''Hey, come on boy, follow Dad''?

Tanata came up behind Sheriff, who didn't move at all when he sensed the man's presence. Sheriff had recognized Tanata by his odor, as easily as if Tanata had shouted his approach from thirty yards away.

Tanata had a big grin on his face. Obviously, he was pleased with something. Just as obviously he had been drinking. There was the feast in honor of the men who would fight tomorrow, the planned attack on the Kindu. ''You must come,'' Tanata insisted.

Sheriff didn't argue. He'd had enough introspection for one day. He stood and followed Tanata back to the center of the village. The drums beat deafeningly—and Tanata laughingly explained to Sheriff that the drummers were beating out a wedding song. They weren't so foolish as to alert the Kindu to their plans.

''And it will be a wedding.'' Tanata laughed again. ''We will wed the Kindu to Lady Death. The bride wears a red dress woven with the blood of her husbands.''

The men sat in the village square, cross-legged, and were waited on by the Fashanti women, all aglow with the special aphrodisiac that rises up when females look at men who are about to fight.

Sheriff took a seat next to Tanata. He listened to the now familiar singsong of the Fashanti language. Not yet fluent, he could follow enough words to know that the men were talking about themselves and the Kindu. Let them think that theirs was the war, theirs the battle. They would never understand the realities of global politics—and there was no reason for them to. They could never comprehend that this was a small production in the theater of world events. If this part of the struggle could be kept on such a small stage, then the world might be spared a larger and more deadly confrontation. Most Americans had no idea where the nation of Leikawa was. It was Sheriff's goal to keep it that way. There were no major military installations—yet. No space-age outposts to defend or attack. Just the Kindu, the Fashanti, three Czechs, and Michael Sheriff, painted blue.

The only inkling the outside world had that all was not right in Leikawa was the announcement of the deaths in the mining camp. The atrocities that Sheriff had witnessed on videotape. But the details had been so garbled, without mention of burnings, of mutilations, of rapes and tortures, that it had been impossible to know whether the deaths had occurred as part of a landslide, a mine cave-in, or even food poisoning.

But if there were many more incidents like that—

"You must enjoy the privileges of a Fashanti warrior!" Tanata exclaimed with a slight slur in his voice. "You will have your choice." His hand swept the semicircle of women that had suddenly congregated in front of Sheriff.

Sheriff, in a genuine way, felt honored. These were considered the six most beautiful young women in Fashata.

The females were all blushing, some covering their mouths with mock embarrassment. Only one was looking directly at Michael Sheriff. Enabia, a young woman who had caught his attention much earlier. She was stripped to the waist, as were all the others. Her breasts were as pert and full as he remembered, her nipples pointing up. The tips of them were rouged with some primitive coloring, drawing his attention directly to them.

Sheriff stood and walked over to Enabia. Her eyes were averted to avoid his direct stare. He took her hand, then walked away, tugging at her arm only a little bit at the very first. Soon she was racing to keep pace with him.

25

HE WAS SPRAWLED on the woven mats of the hut that had been given to him. Enabia was bent over the fire, tending it before joining him. She placed a handful of water-soaked sticks around the perimeter of the tiny fire—their smoke would keep away the mosquitoes and other insects. Sheriff's hands reached down and tore off the small loincloth, leaving him naked. He was already getting hard. When Enabia turned, finally, she saw his erection and smiled hesitantly. She walked over to him and removed her own scant coverings. He moved to drag her down and onto her back, but she resisted, evidently wanting to wait a few moments before assuming that position. Normally that would excite Sheriff. A woman's assertiveness was, in general, highly erotic to him. But not this night, not this time, not here in Leikawa, on the evening before a battle.

He roughly pulled her down, the small shocked sound that escaped her throat an honest expression of surprise. He covered her body with his. Without the usual foreplay he entered her. There would be none of the sensual lingering that Sheriff had employed to bring countless women to their ecstasy. The Fashanti woman was dry at first. At the intrusion, a small whimpered protest broke through her lips. But Sheriff's first thrusts came forcefully and soon there was more than sufficient lubrication.

But as he pounded his pelvis against Enabia's, Michael Sheriff wondered why he needed it this way. Maybe this was the warrior's way, the gladiator's way, the way of the man who is to die tomorrow?

Each of his pulses brought out a shudder of response from Enabia, the air literally forced from her lungs. Sheriff was propped up, his arms held straight. He looked down at the Fashanti woman, examining her expression of commingled pain and pleasure. The assault went on. He gritted his teeth, refusing to allow either of them to find relief in a quick orgasm.

Then—with a decision that formed in him without consciousness—he stopped. He looked down at Enabia's puzzled and frightened face. No, the primeval urge that had overtaken him was no warrior's search for physical and mental release. That wasn't what men were seeking when they had sex before battle. They were merely implanting their seed for perhaps the last time. Taking one more stab for immortality. If the gladiator died tomorrow, trident-speared or lion-mauled, then maybe his seed would sprout in a woman's belly. And one day, perhaps that son of his loins would break the trident, beard the lion.

That's what had been in the back of Sheriff's mind.

But Michael Sheriff already had a son.

Sheriff closed his eyes and collapsed onto Enabia. She held her body rigid and motionless, in fear of what this strange behavior might mean to her. She tried to prepare herself for an attack more savage and painful than the last.

His arms wrapped round her gently—to squeeze the breath out of her, she thought first. But no, he merely lifted her up from the mat. He kissed her. In her surprise at his mouth upon hers, she drew a sharp intake of breath—and the breath came warm and humid out of Michael Sheriff's lungs.

He was still inside her, but there were no more thrusts that pressed her so hard against the grass mats. Sheriff's muscular hips began a smooth and rhythmic motion, a kind of lovemaking Enabia had never experienced with the rough Fashanti who had been her other mates.

Now this man, so palely white beneath the light blue pigment, began to flow in her body, eliciting responses she had never known. She prayed a little prayer to her mother's spirit that the things she felt were not evil, that they were as good for her soul as they felt for her body. But soon, all thoughts of her mother vanished from Enabia's mind. She relaxed into the touch and the smell of Sheriff. Her legs fell apart and lifted in an automatic invitation to him. The man's mouth went down to her throat. His tongue washed her flesh with long, wet stripes. Beyond her control, her body began to call out with a desperate need for release. Lust washed over her. It swept her mind and cleansed her of fear. Enabia's arms clasped the white man's back, her palms flattening against his shoulders. Her belly grew warmer, wetter, hotter and then broke. The unrhythmic waves overcame all her senses. She became a single elongated pulse of desire.

She tried to collapse back onto the mat. But the white man hadn't stopped. Enabia's arms clung to him even more fiercely. He wasn't going to stop! She dragged her nails across his back. Her mouth opened in a new mixture of pleasure and pain. He wasn't going to stop! His hips kept up that gentle insistent intrusion, the teasing withdrawal followed by the forceful insertion. Again the waves began to rise in Enabia, again they broke, again her mouth was flung open, and her legs spasmed with the force of her release.

He moved off her, but not out of her. Puzzled she followed his lead and for the first time in her life discovered herself straddling a male, her knees forced far apart, her wetness flowing down from inside her onto his hairy belly, soaking both of them. She thought he meant to let her go, let her rise, but those hips never ceased moving. They never stopped their thrusting. Again the wonderful, terrifying thought reverberated through her mind. *He wasn't going to stop!*

Her breasts hung down, scraping against the hair on his chest. They swung back and forth to the rhythm of his thrusts. She wanted to bring her legs together, to hold him in tight for a moment—so tight he would have to pause in that rhythm, so she could recover. Never had a man done this to her. When she finally sensed that his seed was bubbling beneath her, that he was about to commence his own violent shudderings, she felt both vast relief and acute disappointment.

It was no wonder that the sex act had a god all its own.

26

"IT'S UNBLENDED WHISKEY," said the Chairman. "Most of what Americans drink is a mixture of different types—usually whatever happens to be on hand at the brewery, I imagine. The best way to take an unblended whiskey is to serve it plain, without ice if possible. But certainly without water, soda, or—God forbid the sacrilege—a mixer."

Katrina brought him the drink—two fingers of unblended Scotch whiskey in a squat crystal glass. Then she brought one to Roger as well. But Roger's contained only a single finger of the liquor.

"Your father, as you may remember from his file, has a preference for Glenfiddich. It's good," the Chairman said, and looked into Roger's eyes with the sense of imparting a valuable lesson on the young, "but he might do better."

That day, just after his morning run, Katrina had announced that Roger would be having dinner with the Chairman that evening. She left no room for argument, and she answered his few questions almost grudgingly. What time would the Chairman come? What should Roger wear? Was there something he should be thinking about beforehand? Was the Chairman going to grade him on anything?

"Grade?" Katrina echoed with smiling contempt. "You are no longer in school. This is life."

Roger was unused to straight liquor, but this smoky whiskey was smooth even to his untrained palate.

"I know," said the Chairman, as he nodded to dismiss Katrina from the room, "that your excursions away from here have been limited to a few trips into town with Katrina—''

Roger had felt like a baby, being chaperoned by a nursemaid. Only the relief of seeing other people, and hearing other voices, overcame his small humiliation.

''—so tonight I thought we should go into Boston for dinner.''

The Chairman stood immediately, and at that instant, the driver of the Chairman's car opened the outside door. Roger hastily raised the glass of whiskey to his lips.

''Bring it along,'' said the Chairman.

The Chairman's automobile was a black BMW with tinted windows. Roger was a touch disappointed. He had expected a Rolls or a Jaguar or something that was obviously very very expensive. It was only when he got inside the car, and they began rolling along the gravel drive toward the gate that Roger realized where all the expense had gone.

It was in the interior of the automobile. Outside it looked like just another black BMW. You saw them on the highway all the time. The windows were tinted dark so you couldn't see inside, but not much else was different. But inside, Roger was sitting on the softest black leather he'd ever felt. It seemed as if he were crushing it, the skin was so soft. The back of the driver's seat held a long tray in the upright position. When Roger looked at it curiously, the Chairman smiled and pressed a button. The tray slowly lowered into position: two telephones, keyboard and CRT, three arrays of switches with code letters beneath them—Roger couldn't begin to imagine what *they* controlled.

But what was most remarkable about the automobile was the ride itself. Roger didn't know, either from the noise or from the motion, when the car was moving or when it had actually stopped. He scoffed at himself for the hours he had spent praising the souped-up cars he and his friends used to drive. Their raw power was obviously inferior to the control of this BMW.

A half hour later they were driving past the Boston waterfront, and a few minutes later the BMW pulled up in front of a restaurant very near Quincy Market. Roger knew where they were, for his father had taken him on a quick tourists' round of the city, and Roger had a good memory for geography.

Roger automatically reached for the door, but stopped short, realizing that the driver was already on his way around. He and the Chairman climbed out of the car. Roger was pleased to note the faces of the curious passersby, who had paused to see who would emerge from a chauffeured car with tinted windows.

He had often done the same thing on the streets of Las Vegas. Peered at limousines to see who was inside. What people looked like who could afford such luxuries. He had many times been part of the gaping crowd.

Now, suddenly, he was on the other side. Being gaped at. The sensation was peculiar. He looked at the Chairman, who took no notice of the crowd, but placed his ebony cane on the brick pavement and nodded in the direction they were to go.

Like the Chairman, Roger's father was on the other side. Because of his job. Because of what he'd done. And what he was. His father would never be part of a gaping crowd, Roger knew that.

Right now Roger wondered: Is this just a taste of what my father feels? Or have I gone over to that other side too?

The restaurant was upstairs. It was called The Ringed Mallard, and it specialized in game. There were people waiting in line to be seated, but Roger and the Chairman were immediately taken to their table by the maître d'. He did not even ask whether they had a reservation. Roger watched his older companion carefully. There must be tricks to how one acted in these places. There would be little things, slight movements, that he should learn. If this were his father, he'd simply ask, but he didn't know exactly how he was expected to behave around the Chairman.

For a place as fancy as this, Roger expected an enormous menu. He was surprised to find it so brief—only a half dozen items, hand-scripted on a single page of parchment set inside a small leather folder. Most of the items were in French—and Roger didn't read French.

"What will you have, Roger?" the Chairman asked.

Roger felt that same dread that came over him in school when the teacher announced a pop-quiz. What was the best guess? Why guess? "You've been here before," Roger said, putting down the menu. "You must know what's good. Would you order for me?"

"Of course," said the Chairman. The old man went back to the menu with relish, as if he were pleased with the opportunity to order double. Roger was amused. He'd had only a little contact with the Chairman, and the man had always seemed imperturbably cool. But evidently, he could get excited about food. Roger had done the right thing. *Remember that,* Roger told himself, *sometimes it's better to admit you don't know instead of putting up a bull front and trying to fake your way through.*

It proved to be a strategy that was more than adequate for the occasion. By letting the Chairman's obvious expertise go to work for him, Roger was able to enjoy one of the best meals he'd ever had in his life. A pâté of layers of goose and bear livers. *Bear!* A Muscovy duck, with succulent dark flesh and a crispy garlic-flavored skin. Tender white asparagus with a very tart mayonnaise dressing that made Roger think he had never tasted mayonnaise before. With vegetables and breads and sauces and seasonings like nothing Roger had ever come across. And for dessert a very simple wedge of chocolate cake—that was so heavy Roger wondered that it didn't tip the table over.

The Chairman had ordered two bottles of wine, a Bordeaux for the main course, and then a sweetish German wine for the dessert. Roger was two years underage for drinking in Massachusetts, and knew he didn't look legal—but there was no question made of that in The Ringed Mallard. One more little example of the Chairman's power—he wasn't the sort of man to whom a waiter said, "May we see your companion's driver's license, please?"

Afterward, the Chairman ordered brandies for them.

Roger watched how the Chairman held the glass with the stem between two fingers, so that the bowl rested in the palm of his hand.

"This warms the brandy," explained the Chairman. "The warmth releases the bouquet."

Roger followed suit. He placed his nose in the bowl of the glass and breathed in—and nearly choked, the odor was so strong and pungent. He touched his tongue to the brandy. Even after all he'd had to eat and drink, the taste seemed to explode in his mouth.

"Roger," the Chairman said suddenly, "this is a business dinner."

Roger stared. It was the last thing in the world he expected the Chairman to say.

"Business?" he echoed. Now he wished he hadn't had anything to drink. Nothing at all. That he were stone cold sober. He even wondered if he shouldn't feel tricked. What did the Chairman have to say to *him* about business?

"I know you read the files on your father," said the Chairman.

Roger nodded.

"And some things in them must have come as a bit of a shock."

Roger nodded again. The East Coast, Roger had found out, was big on understatement.

"Of course, those files didn't contain everything we know about Michael Sheriff. Not by a long shot. They gave you very little indication, I think, of exactly what it is your father does now."

"Since he came to work for you," said Roger slowly. His tongue suddenly felt thick.

"You may discover those things," said the Chairman, "in good time. You may—also in good time—find out a few things about the company which employs your father."

The Chairman glanced to the right and the left. They were in a secluded corner of the restaurant—given a view of the lighted harbor park—but the Chairman's glance suggested that they be very careful in their speech.

"That time isn't yet," said the Chairman. "It would be—" He paused for the right word.

"Dangerous?" Roger suggested.

"Dangerous will do," admitted the Chairman. "Dangerous for you to know much more than you do."

"But I already know—"

"More than most," the Chairman said quickly. "More than most," he repeated, with a pleased smile, as if thinking of all those people in American—and foreign—governments who would give a great deal to know as much about MIS as eighteen-year-old Roger Sheriff knew.

"I don't think my father meant to betray you or anything like that," Roger said hastily. "When he talked to me. And he didn't know what was going to happen in Andy's Surplus that afternoon—"

"Certainly not," the Chairman broke in hastily. "What you know about your father and MIS, I've allowed you to know. Roger, you must have figured out by now that it was I who sent for you."

Roger blinked.

"That it was I who provided the map that allowed you to appear so suddenly on your father's doorstep . . ."

Roger shook his head slowly.

He had thought his father sent the map.

That it was his father's way of saying, *Come to me, son.*

"You mean he didn't want me, he wasn't—" Roger faltered.

"Your father wanted you more than anything else in the world," the Chairman said matter-of-factly. "In fact, I think you were the only thing in the world he really *did* want."

"Then why didn't *he* send for me?"

"You tell me," said the Chairman.

Roger considered. "It's dangerous for me to be around. For me. For him."

"Exactly," said the Chairman.

"Then why has he let me stay?"

"I promised him I would look after you. Your father trusts me, Roger. And he has every reason to, I might add."

"Then why did *you* send for me?" demanded Roger.

The Chairman paused, sniffed his brandy again, tasted it, nodded approval, and then said: "Two reasons. The first is your father. He needed you, and to some extent, it's my business to see that my operatives get what they need. The second reason brings us back where we started."

Roger shook his head. "I don't understand. Where we started?"

"This is a business meeting," said the Chairman. "Or not quite that exactly. It's more in the line of recruitment."

Recruitment.

Suddenly, Roger understood. All of it.

27

AT DAWN the next morning Tanata went urgently through the village asking everyone he saw where the white man had gone. No one had seen Sheriff. When the Fashanti warrior finally found Enabia she seemed dazed and could only murmur that Sheriff had left her some time ago.

Tanata finally discovered Sheriff as he was washing in the small stream that ran close to Fashata. Michael was nude, covering himself in the white suds of soap, scrubbing himself clean of the blue dye. Tanata sat on the bank and wondered at the strange manners of Europeans. Here was one who had embraced the ways of the Fashanti and seemed to have become as much like them as it was possible for any white man to be. He had said that he was honored by the ornamental paint of the Fashanti, and now on the day of the great battle, he was erasing it. He had clothed himself in only a loincloth for six weeks. Now his khaki clothes were carefully laid out on the grass by the river.

Sheriff rinsed himself clean and then walked out of the water. He nodded to Tanata. After drying himself of the river water with a clean rag, he drew on the strange white underclothes the Europeans wore. Tanata had never understood why the Europeans elected to be confined in that uncomfortable disease-breeding way.

Then Sheriff put on his trousers and shirt. Both were of khaki, leaving Tanata with the impression of a soldier's uniform. Sheriff continued by drawing on heavy cotton socks and then the leather boots he had discarded so long ago. As he was tying the laces he began to talk.

"Today I'm going to fight as a white man, Tanata. I'm going to wear the clothes of my own people. I'm honored that you and the rest of the Fashanti have given me the privilege of acting and dressing like one of you. But the fact is, I'm not one of you."

"Why do you say these things?" asked Tanata, wondering what had brought on this change. He wasn't angry but puzzled.

At first Sheriff didn't want to answer. He thought of lying. But he checked himself. Tanata had proven a great friend, a trusted companion. He deserved the truth. "I am going to have to go back to my people. I will have to act like *them*, observe *their* customs. Last night, when I took Enabia, I took her the way a Fashanti would, not the way one of my people would. How a man takes a woman tells him much about himself and his people's customs."

Tanata agreed with a silent nod.

"I am losing myself into the Fashanti, not being a man of my own people."

"Stay." Tanata wasn't going to argue with Sheriff's wisdom, but there did seem to him to be an alternative. "Bring your son here and stay."

Sheriff gazed over the majesty of the savannah that surrounded them. He pictured Roger running through the grass, spear aloft, shield down, learning the honorable ways of the Fashanti. It was a picture that had its obvious attractiveness.

"No," said Sheriff. "My son was not born Fashanti. It would be wrong of me to ask him to give up his own heritage. It is not our place to become Fashanti. It is my duty to allow the Fashanti to continue in their old ways. I have to go back. This," he said, indicating his clothing, "is the beginning of my return."

Tanata embraced Sheriff. "We will be victorious today. You will return to your son."

They walked back to the village where the men were waiting. Sheriff stopped in his hut and picked up the rifle he had brought. Enabia watched as he quickly and efficiently tore it down, cleaned and reassembled it. He had become such a Fashanti that Enabia had expected him to go into battle with the ancient weapons of her people. As she saw him take care of his rifle she understood that he would never return to her, that he would be going back to his people.

When the warriors left Fashata many of the women wept. So too did Enabia. But her sorrow was different. For some reason she knew that the man who had been hers for a single night, Michael Sheriff, would not be defeated. She also knew he would never again hold her in his arms.

Even the proud warriors of the Fashanti were frightened. It wasn't apparent in their eyes, or in the way they advanced with their natural stealth across the West African savannah. But Michael Sheriff had known fear in a thousand disguises, and he smelled it in this place.

The Fashanti had been legendary for their courage in this part of the world. A Fashanti warrior never ran. These men wouldn't either. Michael Sheriff was as confident of that as he was certain that somewhere within the bodies of these proud, tall, black men there lurked a trembling anticipation of brutal, violent death.

Now, through his binoculars, Sheriff could make out the line of uniformed soldiers advancing toward them across the savannah. They came swiftly, obviously unaware of the Fashanti line which would oppose them. A gazelle, caught between the two small but bloodthirsty armies, suddenly bounded up out of the parched yellow grass, and flew gracefully away, unmolested. It wasn't gazelle blood that would dye the plain today.

The Kindu that were approaching had been trained in warfare from their infancy, never introduced to any concept of mercy, or humanity, or human decency. They killed when they were told to kill, and sometimes they killed for the mere exercise of their prowess.

Spaced evenly across the line of Kindu were the three white men that Michael Sheriff intended to rid the world of. They were the three Czechs who had come to Africa to poison the lives of the Fashanti and their neighbors. These men lived without morals. It was little wonder that they had taken up with the Kindu, for they were the civilized counterpart to the pitiless Africans. They lived without reflection, and murdered without mercy.

The Fashanti had every reason to hate these fifty armed Kindu and the three white men who led them. And every reason to be fearful. These very men arrayed before them had weaved in and out of the Fashanti's territory. They had raped the Fashanti women, not sparing even the youngest. Some Fashanti warriors had seen the corpses of their infant daughters ripped apart by the carnal thrusts of a half dozen Kindu warriors. The Kindu had slaughtered every manchild they came across, decimating the next generation of Fashanti warriors. They had stolen the Fashanti stores of grain, and when they could not steal it, they had burned it. They had broken apart the Fashanti gods, and buried the remains under dung. They had enslaved the Fashanti warriors, worked them to the point of collapse, then allowed the Kindu boys to torture the broken men to an ignominious death.

There was no hope for the survival of the Fashanti if they didn't stop the Kindu now.

Sheriff knew what would happen to him if he were captured. In a cold, unfearful way, Sheriff imagined that the Europeans would simply turn him over to the Kindu, known worldwide for the ingenuity of their tortures—and watch.

Sheriff halted the Fashanti line. The well-trained warriors stopped and immediately disappeared beneath the cover of the coarse savannah grass. He quickly estimated fifty Kindu, many of them armed with Czech rifles. He studied the warriors through his binoculars and found something else he didn't like—two deadly Russian AK-47s, accurate to eight hundred yards, and able to operate with automatic or semiautomatic capability. He gauged the range. He glanced at his own line of Fashanti warriors. Only a few carried rifles, and those were ancient. The rest had only handguns. The machetelike knives that swung from the Fashanti waists on cords of animal hide seemed only sad toys. Sheriff wondered if any of his men would have the opportunity of wielding their favored weapons.

It was therefore all up to him.

And to his rifle.

A 30.30 Remington sniper rifle, accurate to a thousand yards, bolt action, with ten bullets to the clip. It was quiet too. Beyond twenty-five yards or so, only a little puff of acrid smoke gave evidence of its having been fired. Sheriff would need that advantage of silence.

He would have very little time to make the line of Kindu vulnerable to the valiant attack he was certain the Fashanti would make.

It was his responsibility to make their charge a fair fight and not the final suicide of Fashanti pride and honor.

Sheriff sighted his targets in the automatic rifle's telescope. If he could take out the AK-47s and then the three Czechs, not only would the leaders and the most awesome weapons be eliminated, but the line would be broken in half. The fifty soldiers would become two groups of less than twenty-five. There were only twenty Fashanti with him. But these men were fueled with the desire to avenge years of systematic genocide. If they could take out one group, Sheriff would handle the second.

He had coached the Fashanti on his plans. The warriors waited silently. Tanata, designated head warrior, stood behind Sheriff and studied him as he took aim. The head warrior's machete lifted almost imperceptibly into the air. The signal for his men to ready themselves for attack. They had to trust this strange white man who had come into their midst, unannounced and unaccompanied. He was their great hope. If they died because of him, at least they would die in battle and do honor to the gods.

The heaven of the Fashanti was populated only by those warriors who had perished bravely in battle.

Tanata had every expectation of shortly finding himself in that Fashanti paradise, surrounded by all his men.

. . . 28

IN SMOOTH, RAPID ACTION, the Remington fired five times.
The sound of the rifle's bolt action—louder than the shots
themselves—were the Fashanti's signal. As they ran across
the grassy plain toward the right-hand half of the opposing
Kindu forces, they realized that there were five men dead,
not just one. Sheriff had sent a single bullet through the bodies of each of five targets.

The Fashanti shouted. This was a great omen.

Sheriff had paused only a moment in his firing. The two
AK-47s were down, and so were two of the East Europeans.
The third had dropped instinctively to the ground when he
realized that his assault line was being fired upon. Sheriff's
bullet had caught a Kindu warrior behind him in the neck.
The warrior, his shattered head flapping to the left as on a
hinge, slipped down into the tall grass.

The last of the Europeans was nowhere to be seen.

Sheriff kept his ground and continued firing. He worked
from the center of the line out toward the front. One by one
the uniformed Kindu soldiers fell to the ground. Sheriff felt
not a shred of compunction or remorse. The Kindu were
godless. Their brains didn't comprehend any divergence of
right and wrong. The Kindu knew only us and them.

The surprise attack had not allowed the Kindu even to understand where the fire was coming from. All they saw was
the small group of Fashanti circling toward their rear. They
foolishly stood their ground and tried to take aim at the
Fashanti warriors concealed in the waist-high grass. The

Fashanti could run huddled along the ground almost as fast as they could have run upright. In the meantime, of course, the Kindu provided perfect targets for Sheriff's calm rhythmic attack.

He bolted, aimed, and triggered automatically. The rifle's steady fire was broken only by the reloading of the preprepared cassettes of ammunition. He shoved the new magazines into place and resumed his shooting stance so quickly that it would have seemed to anyone watching that he had merely paused for a breath, and to gauge the overall picture.

He ignored the faces of the men he shot. The hollow-shelled ammunition erupted in small explosions wherever it bore through human flesh. Skulls crashed open like melons dropped from a height onto concrete. They were the lucky ones, to whom death came instantly.

The moving, shooting uniformed bodies didn't perish as cleanly. Sometimes a shoulder exploded in a burst of blood and fragmented bone. Once, Sheriff aimed at a kneeling rifleman who stood unexpectedly. The bullet ripped through the man's hips and burst in his pelvis. He screamed and lurched upright. The shredded organs of his belly began to sag out toward the ground.

The yellowish green grass of the savannah became tinged with red and white—blood and bone. They were colors familiar to Sheriff. He had seen them in a hundred other places, in a dozen other climates. He had seen that pattern of red and white on snow and ice, in treacherously billowing salt water and on calm mountain lakes, in cool dark caves and burning deserts, in city streets and plowed fields, in slum apartments and suburban homes. It was a pattern like no other.

He hated the pattern, for it spelled Death.

The Fashanti had reached their foe, and their favored machetes came into play.

Although he kept his rifle to his shoulder, Sheriff fired no more. The Fashanti deserved the opportunity to wreak their vengeance on the Kindu.

He watched the carnage through the telescopic site. Leaderless and demoralized, the Kindu were fodder for the Fashanti knives.

With some sort of sixth instinct, developed in a hundred such skirmishes as this one, Michael Sheriff turned the rifle smoothly to the left, well away from the carnage.

There, rising out of the grass a hundred yards away, was the third East European, taking aim at Sheriff with his own rifle.

Sheriff fired twice. The first shot exploded the European's right elbow. The rifle dropped from his grasp. His right forearm dangled on strings of sinew and muscle.

The second shot shattered his right knee. He dropped with a shout of agony into the grass.

He disappeared but the yellow grass waved with his writhing.

Sheriff now considered that his job was done. He put his rifle down on the ground, and reached into his chest pocket for a Sobranie. He lighted it and watched the African gladiators across the plain. Now and then he raised his binoculars to his eyes.

In only another couple of minutes, the last of the Kindu weapons was silent. The distinctive Fashanti warrior-cry had left off in one last triumphant yell.

Sheriff sauntered over to the battlefield. As he drew nearer, the moans of the wounded took over the silence. He counted eleven Fashanti still standing. Four of them bled, none dangerously. There were no Kindu upright. It was an expensive but complete victory.

Tanata and his six unwounded men wandered about in the battlefield, holding their sharpened, still bloody knives out before them. They knelt beside each fallen Fashanti. If he was beyond hope of recovery, the victorious warrior whispered in his comrade's ear—a prayer to the god of the battlefield. Then the victorious warrior thrust his knife into his comrade's belly and twisted it in a ritualized gesture—a gesture by which countless generations of wounded Fashanti warriors had been dispatched on the battlefield. That particular twist of the knife, the warriors believed, was the key that unlocked the gate of the all-male Fashanti heaven.

Very few of the Kindu warriors remained alive. Several of those who did survive killed themselves rather than face the tortures they knew awaited them at the hands of the victors. One Kindu warrior whose hands had been slashed off—and who therefore had no way of doing away with himself—had his genitals carefully sliced away and then pressed down his throat until he suffocated on his own detached manhood.

At the last, Michael Sheriff led Tanata over to where the third East European had fallen. He was alive but unconscious from loss of blood. Sheriff looked at the fallen man and nodded with satisfaction. As he had thought, this was the white man whose face he had studied on the videotape of the Kindu atrocities. This was the man who had tossed the lighted match onto the children in the midst of the gasoline-soaked pyramid.

Sheriff indicated to Tanata, "He is the cause of the Fashanti misery."

Tanata nodded his understanding, and motioned over two warriors.

They brought over water, and carefully roused the East European back to consciousness.

The man looked groggily around. He stiffened when he saw he was in the hands of the Fashanti. Then he cried out, when the pain of his two wounds suddenly overcame him.

"Help me," the man cried out, in Czech, to Sheriff.

Sheriff did not move or speak.

"Help me," the man cried out in English.

"I understood you," Sheriff replied slowly, and in Czech, "the first time."

One of the Fashanti warriors held down Lukas Paloucky's legs, the other his arms. He lay in a pool of his own seeping blood in the crushed yellow grass of the African savannah.

Tanata crouched down beside him, and with the knife that still dripped the blood of Kindu and Fashanti warriors alike, he made a careful triangular incision in Paloucky's belly, cutting through shirt, trousers, belt, and flesh at once. The Czech's body became a canvas on which Tanata painted the Fashanti symbol of war.

The Czech screamed in agony. The warrior holding his arms slipped his foot beneath the East European's head and jacked it up, so that the European was staring down at his own belly.

Laying his knife aside, Tanata pressed his right hand inside the triangular incision in the East European's belly, and in a moment withdrew a coil of small intestines.

Paloucky screamed in horror and pain.

Tanata stood up slowly. The intestines unwound out of the writhing Czech's body. The entrails—more than ten feet of them exposed now—quivered and steamed.

Tanata took up his knife again, and cut the entrails off right at Paloucky's belly.

The victim screamed.

The two warriors released him.

Paloucky jumped and twisted in the mud his blood had formed underneath him. He quivered and was still. Blood seeped sullenly out of the wound in his belly.

Tanata wound the steaming intestines around his neck like a victory garland.

Michael Sheriff lighted another Sobranie.

"Time to go home," he said.

THE PLANE WAS WAITING on the runway. Michael Sheriff's two bags were already on it. He hadn't worn most of the clothes he'd brought. They were probably covered with mildew by now and would have to be tossed. Sheriff sat in the back seat of the single embassy limousine. The driver was a woman—Vera Kormivan. Short and pretty, with a sweet dimpled smile and a twinkling eye and a heart like a lump of coal. The American ambassador to Leikawa, Margaret Durrell, sat next to Sheriff in the back seat, waving away the smoke from his Sobranie.

"Well," she said loudly, "what do you suggest I say to the Czechs about all this? Do you really think they're going to be pleased to hear that an American citizen—one they know used to be in Intelligence—killed three of their operatives here?"

"Bullshit," said Sheriff. "There's no intelligence service in the world that thinks I'm still CIA."

"Christ," moaned the ambassador, catching the eye of her lover in the rearview mirror. "We can't even send the bodies back. Not after what those savages out there did to 'em."

"I thought you and your friends were going to dog my every step, Madame Ambassador. I thought you were going to hound me, make my life miserable. And so on and so on. But I should have remembered—that's how the CIA keeps most of its promises."

The ambassador didn't reply. Her men had lost Sheriff after only two days. But she countered contemptuously: "You're an outdated cowboy, Sheriff. A man lost in time. The day of the private agent went out with the Orient Express. You and your friends back there in Boston better stop reading kids' books, and understand that global politics is something best left to the professionals."

"You'd better ease up on the hairspray. I think it's eating through to your brain," Sheriff said evenly. "It took me six weeks to get the trust of the Fashanti so I could train them to be warriors again. And three days ago, just twenty of those men and I got rid of the single greatest threat to this country's supply of cobalt and uranium. You've been trying to accomplish the same thing for five years. And how much did you spend? Maybe twenty, thirty million dollars? How many people got killed under your operations? Two hundred? Three hundred? And you're trying to give me shit for doing the job you should have gotten done five years ago?"

"You didn't do it for me," snarled Ambassador Durrell. "You didn't do for your country. You did it for your fee. You're just a hired hand, Sheriff. And someday you're going to get into trouble, and when it happens, I just hope I'm around, so I can look you in the eye, and say, 'Sorry— it's hands off.' "

"You know what?" said Sheriff, smiling. "If I believed you, I'd be sleeping a hell of a lot easier from now on. Just knowing your 'company' wasn't going to put its hand in. But you've screwed things up before, and I've got a pretty good idea you and your boys in Washington are going to screw things up again."

The ambassador was silent.

"What's the matter?" said Sheriff. "Haven't figured out a way to take credit for the Fashanti victory yet?"

"Your flight's about to leave," said Vera Kormivan, turning around in the front seat with a dazzling smile.

"We'd hate to have you stuck here in Leikawa another minute."

As he walked up the stairway and onto the big jet, Sheriff turned and flipped his middle finger up at the retreating limousine.

How many times had he sat in the first-class section of a 747 and watched this view? Sheriff looked out at Boston's skyline, so much closer to Logan Airport than most other cities were to their own air terminals. The plane was descending quickly. The stewardess eyed him with some suspicion. He still held his glass of Scotch in his hand, having refused to give it up to her. It was a common though expensive brand of blended whiskey, but what the hell? After what he'd gone through in Leikawa, Sheriff felt he had a right to get a buzz on with rotgut if he wanted to.

The jet's engines roared with protest as the plane braked on the macadam runway. Boston. The place he lived. And now, just maybe, his home.

He continued to sip the Scotch as the 747 taxied up to the International Arrivals building. Sheriff stood, mechanically gathering up his few things, and walked to the front of the plane. He waited for the door to open.

He'd done this so many times he felt as if he were on automatic pilot. Up the ramp and into customs. He traveled so much that he knew the inspectors by sight. And one of them by name. An older man who'd been in the navy. He always let Sheriff straight through. Today, with Sheriff at the head of the line, he was out in no time at all.

Out through the double doors into the terminal, and then over to the parking garage, and then—"Dad."

Sheriff was startled out of automatic pilot. He stared.

"Want me to carry that?" Roger asked.

Someone at the airport. Such a simple thing, really. Didn't it happen to other men? Other *fathers?* Shouldn't a man expect his boy to meet him at the airport after a six-week absence?

Sheriff put his arm around the boy's shoulders, and squeezed.

Of course he should expect it.

DONALD E. WESTLAKE
Writing as
RICHARD STARK

Classic Crime Novels featuring Parker, the fearless steel-fisted hood who will stop at nothing to get what he wants.

"Super-ingenious, super-lethal...Parker is super-tough."
The New York Times Book Review

THE HUNTER   68627-9/$2.50

Doublecrossed by his wife and left for dead after a heist, Parker plots a relentless trail of revenge that leads him into the New York underworld.

THE MAN WITH THE GETAWAY FACE   68635-X/$2.50

Disguised by plastic surgery, Parker is safe from revenge by the Mob, but his plans for a new heist turn out sour when he learns that his partner's girl is out to cross them both.

THE OUTFIT   68650-3/$2.50

After an attempt on his life, Parker decides to settle the score with the Outfit, and goes after the Big Boss with an iron will and a hot .38.

THE MOURNER   68668-6/$2.50

Blackmailed into robbing a priceless statue, Parker figures he can make the crime pay—but he doesn't count on a double cross, a two-timing blonde, and a lethal luger aimed to kill.

THE SCORE   68858-1/$2.75

When an invitation to a heist turns into a plan to rob an entire town, Parker begins plotting a perfect crime that calls for guts, guns, and a whole lot of luck.

SLAYGROUND   68866-2/$2.75

After a heist goes sour, Parker, pursued by a couple of crooked cops and some local hoods, escapes with the loot into a deserted amusement park where all that matters is staying alive.